TWISTED DARKNESS
TALES OF TERROR

New Twisted Tales to Terrorize You

TRACY LA'RAE

Copyright © 2021 by Tracy La'Rae

All rights reserved. No part of this publication may be reproduced, distributed, or transmitted in any form or by any means, including photocopying, recording, or other electronic or mechanical methods, without the prior written permission of the publisher, except in the case brief quotations embodied in critical reviews and other noncommercial uses permitted by copyright law.

ISBN: 978-1-63945-194-4 (Paperback)
978-1-63945-279-8 (E-book)

The views expressed in this book are solely those of the author and do not necessarily reflect the views of the publisher, and the publisher hereby disclaims any responsibility for them.

Writers' Branding
1800-608-6550
www.writersbranding.com
orders@writersbranding.com

Dedicated to my new friend, Reed. May he never be able to walk down a dark hallway without looking over his shoulder.

My ohana, for always believing in me and pushing me to be better.

ArthurO and Charlie, my partners in crime.

Macama, for all the creepy ideas.

Kim, my sunshine, you saved my life. I'm forever grateful.

VOODOO CURSE

Chapter 1

I was running late. I was supposed to be at Noelle's house an hour ago but due to circumstances, my nap ran over or I was late. We made arrangements to get together this evening. Since I was late, I cut through the cemetery. I was halfway through it when I realized I should have brought flowers, so I looked around and borrowed the freshest bunch I could find. "Miss Amelia LaDune. Rest In Peace," had them, written on their graves. A large bouquet of black roses, wow, I've never seen that color before. I bent down and picked them.

"Thank you, Amelia," I said.

Just as I said that I got pricked by one of the rose thorns, then a large crow swooped me and pecked me right over the head, "Stupid bird", I cried out and landed on Amelia's grave. Suddenly the air went completely silent, it was as if the world stood still for a minute. It was five-thirty and the air was scorching hot here in the bayou. The locus gave off a burst of noise and I took off running. The crow followed me relentlessly. Finally, after I exited the cemetery, I stopped and it flew back. I took a left on rue Larae street and followed the sidewalk to Noelle's house.

She looked up, "You're late," as she was playing with her cat. I showed her the roses from behind my back.

"You're forgiven," she smiled.

"How exotic they are, and they smell great. I've never seen black roses before, they're beautiful."

She leaned over and kissed me.

"Oh, you're bleeding!" Am I? I got pecked by a crow on the way here," I said.

"That's odd."

"Yeah I was walking through the boneyard and it swooped me, damn crow."

"It's pretty deep, let's go clean that up." I followed her to the bathroom, she wiped it with some alcohol and put some ointment on it. "All better." She smiled as she hugged me.

We headed downstairs to the kitchen. She grabbed the picnic basket, "I made your favorite, sub sandwiches with extra mayo, plus we had cheese and grapes. Let's go to our favorite spot under the willow tree."

I grabbed a grape and popped it into my mouth, it burst with flavor, it reminded me of kissing Noelle, so yummy. She pulled out a bottle of wine, "Aren't we naughty."

I smiled, "Great with cheese, good thing you packed some."

We laid the blanket down and unpacked the basket. She poured a glass of wine, "To your boo-boo," she laughed as we toasted.

"Mmm smooth." We sat and talked till twilight then we packed up and headed for home. I pulled her in close to kiss her, "I'm so lucky to have you."

"You really are," she teased, "I'll see you tomorrow, goodnight."

Chapter 2

I woke to drums beating, oddly I don't remember that one of the phone's settings. My head was throbbing. I rubbed it and I had bumps all over my scalp. I ran to the bathroom mirror to see what's going on, it felt like craters.

"What the freak!" I looked closely at my head with the mirror, "Freaking crow gave me something!"

At least no one can see them. I got ready for school and went down to get breakfast, eggs, and toast with grape jelly on it. I was getting up when mom came up behind me and patted me on the head like she always did.

"What in the world!? What did you get into to cause this?" she asked.

I told her about the crow and she said, "It should go away in a day or two."

I hope she was right because they really hurt.

I rode my bike to school and met Noelle and Kokouia, Noelle's best friend. I told her what mom said about the bumps and headed to class. By lunchtime, I thought my head was on fire. They hurt so bad. Noelle kept yelling at me for touching them. Later, Noelle told Kokouia about the black roses and she did the sign of the cross across her chest then spat over her shoulder. She said nothing and looked at Noelle, " Well that's strange, I wonder where he got them."

Noelle questioned, and then they looked at me. I sat there in silence ignoring them thinking about my head, it was driving me crazy.

By the end of the day, I raced home and hit the shower, the cold water felt amazing. I would have stayed there longer but mom came knocking on the door yelling about the water bill. Things have been tight since dad died.

I yelled back, "I'm getting out now."

Then stayed there another five minutes then turned off the shower, and got out. "Please let them be better by tomorrow," I said as I looked in the mirror. I got dressed in my pj's and headed downstairs to the kitchen. I could smell dinner cooking as soon as I hit the stairs. I walked into the kitchen and mom was standing by the stove stirring a pot.

"What's for dinner mom?"

"One of your favorite beef stew and fresh bread that I made from scratch, it's almost done."

"How's the head?" she asked.

"Better since I showered."

I grabbed an cookie from the dolphin cookie jar and it chirped out happily.

"Don't fill up on cookies now," she warned.

I set the table and grabbed the tea and glasses.

"Sun tea, you can't go wrong with sun tea," I said as I poured it. The timer oinked and mom pulled out the bread. She taped the pan and the bread popped out in a perfect loaf.

"Grab the butter please will ya."

"Sure thing mom."

I placed it in the middle of the table and sat down. Mom filled our bowls withs stew as I sliced the bread. The kitchen smelled heavenly. We talked about our day and each had seconds of stew. By the end of dinner, we were stuffed.

I put away the leftovers and headed to the family room to watch tv. We watched our favorite Thursday night programs. By bedtime, I kissed mom, said goodnight then headed to bed. I fell asleep in seconds. I dreamed of ritual drums beating and a shadow man dancing. Twirling around and around, his eyes went back in his head, the whites of his eyes glistened as the firelight hit them. The drum's rhythmic beat went on. He went faster and faster as he danced then suddenly he stopped.

Chapter 3

The alarm blared in my ear, I smacked the button and felt immediate pain through my hand.

"What the hell?" I turned the light on and was shocked at the sight.

Every fingernail was black and the puss was seeping out of it. I looked at it closely, "Oh my God what's happening?!!"

I yelled. My mom knocked on the door, "Are you okay in there? What's going on in there?"

"I'm okay, mom, sorry I scared you." I looked down at my hand and shook my head.

"What's going on with me?"

"Be down in ten," I yelled through the door.

I grabbed my clothes and threw them on, grabbed my bag, and went straight downstairs.

"What do you want for breakfast ArthurO?"

"I think I'll skip breakfast this morning, I'm running late already."

"See you after school," she smiled.

"Have a good day." I rode my bike to Noelle's house, maybe she'll know what to do.

I got there and knocked on the door, pain stung through my hand. Her mom answered the door, "ArthurO you know you don't have to knock just come on in." she smiled.

"Thanks. Is Noelle ready?"

"She's just finished up breakfast now."

"Thanks, Mrs.C."

I walked into the kitchen and grabbed Noelle, "Come with me please."

I said to her, "Okay, what's up?" She looked worried.

We walked to the porch and I showed her my hands.

"GROSS! What in the world did you do? Omg! Are you gonna be alright?" She has a worried face now that she looked at them.

"I don't know!" she went into the house and came back with gloves, "Here wear these, it'll cover them up. What are we gonna do with you?" she sighed.

At the end of the day, I managed to hide them from everyone. I dropped Noelle at Kokouia's house then went straight home. I headed straight up the stairs. I looked at myself and I was a mess. There had to be a reason for all of this and I needed to find out soon, possibly before I look like a leper.

Chapter 4

That night I dreamed of smoke, I filled the air, I saw women chanting all dressed in white. They were spinning chanting as they went in the sink with the drum beats.

A snake danced over the head of the shadow man. The drums got louder and louder, the shadow man looked right at me and smiled a twisted smile. He looked deep into my soul. Then reached out for me, I woke coughing the smell of fire permeated the air. I looked out the corner of my eye and saw the outline of a man. It moved toward me. I moved to the light and it was gone.

I got up dreading what I might find. I didn't notice anything new until I took off my shirt and saw flaking skin. I did a head shake and went downstairs, had breakfast, and went to school. All through the class, I was itching like a bear on a tree. The bell rang and it was lunchtime, I headed to my locker and grabbed my lunch. Then headed to the cafeteria. I sat down next to Noelle and Kokouia. I slowly ate but kept on itching and wiggling around.

"What's wrong with you? You got ants in your pants." Noelle teased.

"I'm so itchy! It's driving me crazy."

"Here let me look at it." She lifted my shirt to look. I knew something was wrong when she jumped back.

"What? What's wrong?"

"Your back is full of scaly areas, you look like a snake shedding."

Kokouia gasped. "What the hell did you get into?"

"I don't know, but it's getting worse every day. It's something terrible."

I had tears in my eyes, I was looking back as I felt.

"It's okay, let's focus on lunch." Noelle said, "And change the subject."

Kokouia smirked with her head shaking. At the end of the day, I told Noelle that I wasn't feeling well and went straight home. I stepped into the doorway and headed for the shower, maybe the water would make me feel well. I was tired of hurting and itching. I turned on the water and waited for it to get hot and pulled my clothes off and got in. It felt so refreshing. I closed my eyes as the water dowsed me, suddenly I heard something in the bathroom.

"Hello? Mom, is that you?"

No one answered. I pulled the shower curtain back closed. I smelled smoke and watched the shadow move past the curtain. I pulled the curtain back again, nothing was there.

"I'm losing my mind." I turned off the shower, got out, picked my towel up and something fell. I bent down to pick it up, it was a puka shell.

"Where did that come from?"

I put it on the corner and got dressed. I looked in the mirror and saw the shadow man's face smirking at me, then his arms flew out at my throat. I was gasping as his laughter filled the air. The lights went out without warning. I fell to the ground flailing around. I heard a knocking sound.

"ArthurO are you okay in there?" All of a sudden he was gone.

Mom yelled "ArthurO seriously are you okay? I'm coming."

She opened the door, "What are you doing in here?" she asked.

"I'm alright, I just fell that's all." I said I didn't want to worry her.

"Well get up, dinner will be done in a few." She looked worried.

"I'm fine mom," As I got up.

"Okay, see you downstairs." and she left.

I looked in the mirror, "What the hell was that?" I grabbed my clothes and left.

Chapter 5

At lunch the next day I told Noelle and Kokouia what might be causing my misfortune.

"Remember when I got pecked by the crow when I got you flowers?"

"Yes, what about it?" Noelle answered.

"Maybe that crow had some kinda disease or something." she looked at me thinking—

"Well I guess that could happen."

"When'd you get peaked by a crow? Watchya be doing hanging around them in the first place?" Kokouia asked.

"Remember when he got me roses the other day- I told you about them, they were black roses."

Kokouia stood did the sign of the cross and spat over her shoulder, "What was that all about?"

We both asked her but she didn't answer.

"Did ya get pricked by one of the roses?" she stared at me.

"Oh ya, I forgot about that, yes, yes I did."

"You be pickin' roses of a grave?" she looked serious.

I shook my head yes, Noelle looked at me disappointed.

"Well, that was bad, real bad. Stealing from dead people," Noelle said.

"I think I know what's wrong with ya- do you remember who you've taken them from?" Kokouia asked me.

"Yes, Ameila LaDune." I said.

"The voodoo queen! Only them be havin' black roses on their graves." She made the sign of the cross again.

"Some of them be more powerful after death." She sounded serious.

I laughed nervously, "What's she cursing me? Is that what you're telling me?"

They both were staring at me.

"Ooh you are in deep trouble now, Miss Amelia LaDune was one of the most powerful voodoo queens that ever lived. You ain't got a chance now. My mamas gonna flip when I tell her whatcha done." Kokouia crossed her arms then spit and walked away.

"Man, what did I do? You really believe in all this stuff?"

"I think you're in deep trouble. We're gonna have to figure out how to uncurse you. I'll see if Kokouia's mom will help us. She's into voodoo herself, I know she can help, I'll catch up with you later. Try not to do anything else." then she was gone.

I just sat there staring at my lunch, that's when I noticed a large worm crawling through my sandwich.

"Aaahhh what the freak!?"

I lifted the bun and there were several there crawling. I left it there and went to class.

Chapter 6

The alarm went off, climbed out of bed, my mouth tasted terrible. I grabbed my toothbrush and started brushing. When I spit out the toothpaste the sink was covered in blood. I looked in the mirror, my gums were bleeding. I shook my head and decided to stay home. I already look like the living dead. I pulled my sweatshirt off and went back to bed.

I dream of the shadow man again. This time he grabbed me and he started chanting, he grabbed me with his hands he looked sinister. The drum beats faster than he blew powder on my face.

I sat straight up awake, freaking out. There was white powder all over my face in bed and I was covered in bed. Thank God mom was at work already.

So I did a load of laundry and treated the stains so mom wouldn't know, then texted Noelle and told her to stop by after school. I decided to search the internet to see what I can find out about Ameilia LaDune and voodoo curses.

Amelia came over with her mother Sukenia on a slave ship. They were sold to an owner named Galven Espitia, six months later he died of a mysterious affliction- then he bled to death. The owner's wife treated Amelia and Sukenia with respect and even evolved with voodoo herself. Together they were a powerful trio. The wife gave them freedom and they continued to live together.

By the time Amelia was eighteen, she was completely lethal. Soon Amelia married doctor Seta and had a daughter. She and doctor Seta were the leaders of the group of followers.

They had a daughter Sauri, but she and Amelia were murdered by a group of white men who attacked the house. The men hung them by their necks in a tall oak tree outside of their house. Soon it was said, the Seta cursed all the men and murdered them.

Within a week, all of them suddenly died of strange and painful afflictions. Amelia and Sauri were buried and a curse was put on their graves to anyone who would disturb it.

"I'm in big trouble now, that's a powerful curse. How am I ever gonna get rid of it?"

I heard drum beats coming from the kitchen. I got up to see what was happening when I noticed on the counter there was a snake in a bowl of blood slithering around. The drums got louder and saw shadows moving all around me. I looked up and the shadow man jumped down from the fridge on top of me. He was laughing his creepy laugh. He spoke words I couldn't understand then blew in my face. I screamed and closed my eyes.

Just then the doorbell chimed, I looked up and all I saw was a snake slithering across the floor and the smell of smoke remained.

"He's getting stronger, I can feel it," after I explained to Noelle and Kokouia. Kokouia told me that she spoke to her mom who is a descendant of Amelia's family. She said that it would take a powerful spell to undo the hex that was placed on me and there were no guarantees it would work.

"My mama has deep issues with us for disturbing her ancestors grave, I'm surprised she didn't put a hex on you herself, but thats a chance you're gonna have to take."

After they left I was all alone with my thoughts, "I'm in deep doo doo," I sighed.

I went to the kitchen to see about something to eat. It had to be soft because of my gums. I settled on a banana. I unpeeled it and took a bite. I spit it out fast, it was black and covered in bugs. I decided on a ginger ale instead.

Chapter 7

By late afternoon, I was nervous and pacing the floor waiting to see Kokouia's mom. I was worried that she wouldn't help me cause I deserved it for taking Amelia's rose, "What if she curses me too?" I tried to calm myself down.

I grabbed a popsicle, after a few minutes I noticed there was something in it. I looked at it closely, a huge frozen slug was in it!

"Gross!" I yelled as I threw it in the sink.

Just then I thought maybe it was part of the curse the bug in my food so I starve to death to finish the job. I was contemplating about it when I heard Kokouias's voice outside. They came in the front door.

"Wow! You look terrible!" Kokouia said.

"Thanks."

"Are you ready to meet my mama? She's waiting for us to come. Let's get a move on."

I left a note for my mom then locked the front door and we all headed to Kokouia's house. I was scared to death she'd tell me I deserve all of this.

On the way, we discussed what's all been going in with me. We all agreed that picking the rose was the worst thing I ever did. I should have known better than to be so disrespectful. Maybe I did deserve all of this curse to make sure I learned my lesson.

We were halfway there when I noticed the shadow man across the street from me. At first, I thought I was just imagining him but then he was right in front of me. No one else seemed to notice him. He had black eyes, they stared right through me. He reached for me just as I jumped backward.

"What's wrong with you? Did you see him again?"

"He was right there, didn't you see him?"

I said, "He had black eyes!" I said excitedly.

"Who? The shadow man? I didn't see no one," Kokouia said.

"Me either." they both just stared at me.

"It's gone anyways, let's just keep walking."

I rushed us up the street hoping he was truly gone.

Chapter 8

Kokouias house was a huge 2 story mansion. It had been handed down for generations. The enormous windows that looked like they were staring at me. Kokouia's mom met us at the front door. She had been waiting for us to arrive. I noticed there was a salt strip across the doorway.

Kokouias mom, S'cie, came up to me and said, "Stand still and hold out your arms."

She took out a feather and a bag of bones and shook them above my head and all the way down my body as she said, "Rid this curse forgiveness true open up the house to you." Over and over.

They asked me to step over the salt. I was hesitant but did what she said. S'cie showed us to the paler room and told us to wait quietly.

She came back, "Now my young one you are telling me what you are doing stealing Amelia's roses?"

I explained how it happened and why I took them. She listened quietly then stood up, did the sign of the cross, and spit over her shoulder.

"You are a fool to disrupt her slumber! You brought then upon yourself you did." she stood there looking at me.

"I'm so sorry. I should have never done it. Forgive me and my stupidity. I'm truly sorry to bring pain and disturbance to her."

S'cie looked at me studying me and my body language then said, "Enough- you be truly sorry or not?"

Her eyes burned into me, "Yes I'm sorry! I wish I could take it back."

I had tears in my eyes. She stood in silence thinking then she spoke, "You be truly sorry- I'll be helpin' ya."

Over the next two hours, she explained what we would have to do to unbreak this hex and how all of this would work. She told us, "The curse be strong it be—I can feel it. The shadow mans beside ya when you walk in the house. You be eatin' or it be tainted to?"

"Tainted? Oh yeah like the bugs in all my food? Then yes!"

"Powerful hex—hard to be breaking. We'll need a sacrifice to offer," she looked at Kokouia and Noelle.

"No! Not then!" I yelled.

"Of course not—be silent! Let me think. You be knowin' where to go Kokouia?" she said.

Kokouias nodded, "Noelle you be lovin' him enough to be helpin'? Your bond must not break or the curse can't be undone."

"Yes, I love him scaly and bloody I still love him. What can I do?" she asked.

S'cie explained to everyone what we must do. Everyone had a job to do to unbreak this curse. She sent us on our way with our orders.

We left the house and were halfway to Noelle's house when she looked at me and said, "I really do love you."

She bent over and kissed me.

Chapter 9

That night I laid in bed my mind consumed with thoughts of what was going to happen. The drums beat rhythmically all around me.

On the floor, there was a salt circle around the bed. S'cie stood there with her bowl and a chicken in the other hand. She looked at me and smirked then slit the neck of the chicken. Blood spurted out of it, it sprayed my face and body. She shook it then went to the alter the blood poured onto the bowl as she fell to her knees covered in blood, she called out to me, "You be sorry? You must truly be the ancestors be waiting."

She bent over to grab my hand, a slit down the middle blood dripped onto the altar. I looked at Noelle and Kokouia they were speaking another language their eyes rolled back into her head. The shadow man stared at me, he waited for S'cie then grabbed my wrist and shook my hand, blood running onto his arm. He looked into my eyes—his black eyes burned into mine. I was scared. I felt helpless. Still, he shook me violently he laughs hysterically.

"Beep beep beep!"

The alarm broke my dream. Thank God! I took a deep breath.

"Breathe, it's okay." I said to myself, "Just breathe."

"ArthurO! You awake in there? I have an early meeting at work. I leaving now," Mom called up to me.

"Okay, mom. I'm up and getting dressed now." I yelled back.

"I made cinnamon rolls. Enjoy!"

I heard the door slam. I looked in the mirror, I looked like death had warned me. I'm sure I couldn't keep hiding from my mom much longer. This had to end and end soon. I gathered all the things I could think of for the ritual later that week.

S'cie said I needed to think really hard about what I wanted to be as a true offering of myself. I went over and over of what I thought would work but in the end, I didn't think any of it was good enough.

After school Kokouia and Noelle came over and showed me what they were gonna use in the ceremony. Kokouia picked up a live chicken from her uncle's house to use to wake up the ancestors. She also made a bag of gris to appease them as well.

Noelle told me she was going to offer a love token of hers to hopefully get the ancestors in insync with what was about to happen. She also offered her a pink diamond ring that I saved for months for her. I thought to myself hard about what would work. I cut a piece of my hair and my father's baseball hat that he left me when he died two years ago.

It was my most treasured possession. If it was good enough nothing was. We headed to S'cie's house. I'd been worrying about the whole ritual all day, what if it didn't work? What if I was cursed enough that I'm just gonna die from it. I was truly sorry but what if the ancestors couldn't tell or didn't care? So many questions in my mind it was hard for me to focus.

Chapter 10

Later that night I hustled up the stairs telling my mom I had a report that was due tomorrow and I'd be working on it all night. I threw off my sweatshirt and stood there looking out the window with a million questions running through my brain still. I heard a mom coming up the stairs so I bolted into the bathroom before she got there. The one place she'd never enter. Knock! Knock!

"What's up mom?"

"I brought you up some brain food. I'll put it on your desk. Holler down if you need anything."

"Thanks mom, love you!"

"Love you more," she said.

I came out of the bathroom to see what she brought me, Mmm… Lots of yummys. Cheese, grapes, peanut m&m's, and a glass of raspberry tea, my favorite. Mom really is a great mom, she's had it rough since dad's passing. Now it's just the two of us and she has to be both parents. Not to mention that she has to work now. It's been an awakening. I can tell she's worn out sometimes, but she always puts on a happy face for me and takes great care of me. Once a week I cook dinner for her, it's our special night together.

Saturday morning I got up early and decided to go back to the cemetery and look at Amelia's grave. I thought maybe there would be a hint of what she'd like in life there. When I was there before, I'd noticed several things sitting around by her grave. I still haven't come up with what I should offer to appease her.

I grabbed a quick breakfast bite and had a cup of coffee. I got my backpack and walked to the graveyard. I followed the path until I reached Amelia's grave. There were fresh-cut black roses in her urn. I stood there staring at the tombstone wondering what I could give her to pay homage for what I did wrong.

Then it hit me. Oxtail soup and corn cakes, a specialty from Africa. It'll be hard to find the ingredients but maybe she'd appreciate the gesture. Also some banyas for dessert. I read she had a sweet tooth. I said I was sorry to her several times as I stood there looking. Just then a black cat came up to me, the grave keeper it's said to be.

"Hi, guys you hungry? I brought some food in case I saw you."

I said as I reached in my bag and pulled out a baggy full of cat food. I poured it out on the ledge of the tombstone. The cat meowed happily then started eating. I lit my candle and left it burning saying goodbye. I pet the cat and walked away.

At least I had a better idea of what I should do now. I walked over to the butcher shop looking for the ingredients for oxtail soup. The man at the store told me to go to the store downtown, he'd have it for sure, he specialized in ritual foods. I went home to grab my bike. I'd be peddling myself to the store, it took about twenty minutes to get to the other butcher shop. There was a long line by the time I got there. I waited patiently until my turn. The man took one look at me and asked who cursed me.

"Mrs. Amelia LaDune."

He stepped back and did the sign of the cross over his chest then spit over his shoulder, "You gonna make oxtail soup? You're gonna need a lot more to appease her than that. I got what ya need." he said.

He grabbed all the ingredients for the soup then went back into the back room and came out with a heart of the ox, an eyeball, and genitals.

"You be needin' to call out all the ancestors to uncurse you-whatcha did upset the spirits of the whole family. Take this. Who'll be helpin' ya?" he asked.

"S'cie," I said.

VOODOO CURSE

"She be good. She forgiving you? You need her on your side. She be strong in the spirit world. Good luck!" he spat over his shoulder once again as I took the package.

I peddled home, I went straight to the computer after I put my package away. I looked up how to make oxtail soup and corn cakes. After searching the internet for an hour I finally found the kind that African people eat for ritual soup on some voodoo site.

I headed downstairs to print off the instructions and get a snack, hopefully without bugs! I decided on a peanut butter and honey sandwich with soup. I sat down with my recipe and started reading. I took several bites of my soup before I looked down and I was disgusted. There were grubs wiggling around in it and my sandwich had half of a roach in it! I spit out my mouthful - this curse is horrible, I'm gonna starve to death.

I'd already lost several pounds due to it. Just then I heard a noise coming from the closet. I got up to see what was going on. When I opened it the shadow man grabbed me by the throat and pushed me backward. I fell to the ground gasping for air. He sat over me laughing, his eyes rolled back into his head as he started chanting. I tried to escape but his grip was too strong. Suddenly everything went black.

Chapter 11

I woke up coughing with my hands around my neck, "What the freak?"
I sat up then pulled myself up off the floor. I had enough of this curse. I looked like a monster and now I'm attacking myself. What's next? The doorbell rang I slowly walked to the door and answered it.

It was the girls, "You ok? You look shaken up!" Noelle hugged me.

"Just having a moment. I'm ok now."

"Here's your homework for the week, everyone's wondering what's wrong with ya. I told em that you had the puke flu no one ever wants details then."

"Smart thinking Noelle"

"Thanks!" I said with a hug.

"You be lookin worse," Kokouia said.

I ignored her remark and said, "I figured out what I'm doing for my appeasement for Amelia, oxtail soup and corn cakes. I also got eyeballs, heart, and genitals to go with them." I smiled at her.

"Mmmm... eyeballs and genital heart soup! Sounds delicious! It's a very special ritual soup and hard to make too." Kokouia added.

"You got directions u do?"

"Found them on the internet on a voodoo site. The man at the butcher shop got all the ingredients for me. He speaks very highly of your mom."

"She da best!" Kokouia smiled.

"We got our special things ready too were getting blood eggs from my uncle sala's house they be very rare them are."

"Great so were all set for the ritual tomorrow? Good thing to I'm starving to death and the shadow mans freaking me out." I said with a grimace.

"He be getting stronger every day. If we don"t rid this curse soon he'll be collecting your soul." Kokouia said very matter-of-factly.

"What? Are you kidding right?" I looked at her and Noelle. Noelle looked at her feet trying to avoid eye contact.

"Apparently it's true S'cie told us the other day after you left. We didn't want to tell you. We knew it would only upset you more." She looked up sheepishly at me.

"Great! I don't imagine he's taking me to heaven either huh?"

"Nada- you be straight to hell."

"Fabulous! Anything else you all forgot to tell me about?" I looked them both in the eyes.

"No," they said in harmony."

Well, that's good." I shook my head at them.

"Here my mama wants us to fill this paper out for the ceremony." She unfolded the paper from her rucksack and handed it to me.

As I looked it over I noticed some of it was very strange and written in another language. But I'm sure the whole ritual will be unusual. So I tried to keep an open mind. Kokouia handed me another paper that had a voodoo blessing on it. I was to read it before I went to sleep three times, then follow the instructions.

Turn once in every direction. North. South, East, and West inside the salt circle. Then place the rock S`cie gave me in the bowl with water and honey. Then light the white candle and place it inside the bowl of water with the rock. Then read the blessing over three times. I then exit the circle through the south side and let the candle burn out on its own. It's supposed to keep the shadow man away through the night. So I'll be stronger for the ritual tomorrow.

I thanked Kokouia and told her to pass it on to S'cie as well. I knew what to do now so she said goodnight and that I'd see her tomorrow at Kokouias place and we'd all walk to the gravesite together. It had to be done at midnight on a Saturday under the full moon. Noelle and

I hung out and watched a movie up in my room until she had to go home. Her dad came and picked her up at eleven pm.

    I kissed her goodnight and told her I'd see her tomorrow night. My mom was asleep in front of the TV so I turned it off, locked all the doors, and headed up to bed. I was really on edge about tomorrow night. What if it didn't work? What if's came looming in my mind like a freight train. Especially knowing I could go straight to hell!

Chapter 12

The day crawled as the minutes turned into hours. I'd gotten up early to make oxtail soup and corn cakes. It was a long and tedious recipe that took hours to make properly, not to mention the horrible smell that I had to endure while it simmered.

Finally, by eight pm it was finished. I put it in a Tupperware container and packed it to go. I gathered all the items I'd be taking with me in my rucksack and placed them carefully by the door. I left a note for my mom apologizing for the smell saying it was a science experiment that went horribly wrong and told her I'd be late.

I was going to Noelle's house with a group of friends so she wouldn't worry. I rolled up on my bike to Noelle's house where we sat around talking trying not to think about what was about to happen. We played cards to kill time.

"Gin!" Noelle said as she slapped down her cards.

"That's five in a row, you're not even trying."

"I'm sorry I'm just nervous about tonight. So many 'What ifs' going over in my head."

"Well, it's getting late, let's go ahead and head over to Kokouia's house, I'm sure they are ready as well by now," she smiles trying to put me at ease.

"It's gonna be alright. It's all gonna work out according to the plan." With that we grabbed everything and walked to her house. We walked slowly since I was dragging my feet to stretch it out, finally we arrived at her front porch. We rang the doorbell and waited for someone to answer. "It's about time we were wondering where you be at," Kokouia stated as she answered the door.

"Well, we're here now and we're all ready to face the music."

"Is everything ready for the ritual?" we asked in unison.

"I got the oxtail soup and corn cakes in my bag," I said as I slapped it.

"Mama's getting the last of the things together now. Then we'd be ready to head out. You look kinda ashy, no worries mama's gotcha." She smiled at me. God, I sure hope so I thought.

A few minutes later S'cie had all of the ritual things packed and was ready. The girls grabbed their bags and we all headed out. We walked in silence under the full moon. We stopped just as we were about to enter the graveyard and lit our candles. We walked in a line till we got to Amelia's tomb.

S'cie has been coming here for years so she knew exactly where to go. She made a salt circle around us that was to protect us from evil spirits during the conjuring. She placed the candles in the middle of the circle and when she lit the candle the flames turned black.

She sprinkled it with gris-gris then chanted, "By the power that be~ we ask to release thee," She grabbed the other candles lit them and placed them on the crept that were serving as an ancestral altar.

She stripped me down to my boxers as she set up the altar. She placed the oxtail soup and corn cakes on the ledge of it, as she said, "We ask Amelia LaDune to step forward and accept our offering," as she did this she lit a purple candle.

"Come forth, come forth with love." the girls chanted as they placed a shell necklace around my neck.

"Come forth come forth with love," they said again as they walked around me sprinkling me with honey.

S'cie pulled out the chicken from the bag and with her dagger she chanted, "We cometh to ya Amelia set free to be—" she then cut the chicken's head off, blood spurted out as the girls collected it in a metal bowl. Then took the feet of the chicken and started marking me down my arms.

VOODOO CURSE

They took their fingers and smeared blood all over my face in a cross above my eyes as they chanted, "Come forth and be-come forth and be!" over and over. I started feeling like I was falling deeper and deeper into a tunnel.

Just then I saw the shadow man, he was dancing around me laughing, dancing round and round. My head was spinning. Kokouia took the bowl of blood and raised it above my head.

S'cie and Noelle grabbed onto it and the three of them dumped it over my head. A flash of lightning ran through my mind. "The powers that be come forth times three we sacrifice thee," they danced with the shadow man around me.

I watched everything in a trance but I couldn't move. The shadow man took the ox's heart and held them above his head then bite into it, intense pain ran through my body. I fell to the ground convulsing all over. They danced around me, their eyes went white up into their heads in a trance-like state, the shadow man chanted, "I step forward to exchange thee, by the powers that be exchange thee, exchange thee, exchange thee," then everything went black.

Chapter 13

I don't know how long I was out. When I woke my body ached all over, my eyes were blurry and I had a headache.

It took a minute for me to shake off what happened finally I looked up at Kokouia and S'cie they were smiling at me as they helped me up. I leaned on S'cie until I could stand on my own.

"How ya be feelin' my love?"

I shook my head to clear my thoughts, then I spoke, "It's gonna be a minute to get used to a new body. How I be lookin'?"

"You look good doctor Seta. You be whiter than before, my love."

S'cie smiled Kokouia looked at me then wrapped her arms around me. "I be waitin to do that!"

"Welcome back grandpa, we missed you!" Noelle handed me a mirror, I looked at myself, "Well i'll gonna be taking a while to get used to this."

Noelle looked at S'cie and said, "See, I told you everything would work as planned."

"Finally, it be awhile what took ya so long? I told you I wanted a black body," doctor Seta said.

"Grandpa, you know only the white boy be believing now!"

"It suits ya my love and soon Amelia be joinin' ya again." S'cie smiled.

"We already have a suitable match- it's just a matter of time." Noelle told them.

VOODOO CURSE

"You be da best voodoo priestess yet."

S'cie hugged Noelle and Kokouia, "It's all about believing and they always believe."

Take a look back at the two stories that started it all.

Beware: not for the faint of heart.

Journey into the terrors and horror that followed the lives of Wilheim in They Return and Rainey in Lulu of the Red Market. Enjoy and be scared.

Scream. Run. Hide.

They might come after you.

THEY RETURN

For my ohana—a special shout out to my crazy kids Big Booty Judy, No Boobie, Bayli Bird, and Sassy Lassie. Thanks for all the fun times. Thanks to my parents who are the greatest parents anyone could ask for. For my Twisted Family, thanks for all the gruesome horror ideas, here's to another bloody season. For Charlie who listens to all my wacky notions and still encourages me to be my eccentric self—I love you all.

Chapter 1

I woke to the sound of birds singing outside my window. There was a light breeze blowing softly through my curtains as I laid there waking up. I was laying there thinking about school when it hit me, in exactly one week I will be 18. I'll finally be stepping into the glorious world of adulthood, with new rights, driving privileges, and the right to speak my mind and have someone actually listen.

I've been counting down the weeks to this transition for months. Mom says I'll have a whole new set of rules and an attitude to back it up, I think she's right. Dad's super excited about the attitude thing the most I think. One good thing they're both looking forward to is that they won't have to drive me all over anymore and I won't have to take the train all the time anymore.

Finally I will have a driver's license- freedom, which is the greatest present of all for my age! Growing up's been rough since I'm the only kid, there's no one to be compared to, no one to give me warnings about things and my parents freak out about everything.

I've been conditioning them for months to calm them down and let me have some room to grow so hopefully on my birthday we can all relax and enjoy ourselves.

They have agreed to let me have a huge party in the garden haus so it should be fun. The garden haus is a few blocks away from our house in the city, it's a large one-roomed house that we head to whenever we want to get away from the chaos of city living and things to relax. There's a large pond by it that you can swim in, fish or boat, lots of trees and flowers, a lot of Germans have them. I live in Germany, we moved here when I was 7, Dads in the military.

So far it's been an adventure. The law's, attitudes and the way people parent is completely different but I embrace it full heartily.

BEEP! BEEP! The alarm went off waking me from my thoughts just as mom called up. "Wilhelm, you're gonna be late if you don't get moving!"

"I'm up mom."

School started in 25 minutes so quickly I grabbed my rucksack, threw on some clothes and headed downstairs. I grabbed the toast mom put out and a water bottle as I headed for my bike. I rode it every morning to school.

Basically I rode it everywhere except when I grabbed the train instead. It takes 12 minutes to get to school from my house so I headed out. I met up with my friends halfway there.

"We're running late today, let's hustle! Eile Eile, ich liebe dich!"

We all started laughing. It was our inside joke between us. It means "Hurry! Hurry! I love you." A few months ago when we were out at the pub Steffi got drunk and kept saying it to people.

Matthias and Steffi are my best friends; we've done everything together since we were little kids. Matthias is 6-foot 4-inches and is a soccer player; we play on the same team, he's the forward and I'm the goalie. He's lighting fast and has super stealing ability; thanks to that we're number one in the district.

He also has a great sense of humor, we bounce off each other; He's full of life and lives it to the fullest. We're also like brothers and would do anything for each other.

Steffi is the serious one of the group, very intellectual. Our job is to make sure she has some fun once in a while. If ever I needed to look at life differently I'd just ask Steffi. She always has her homework for the month done in 4 days and does extra credit.

THEY RETURN

I and Matthias get lectures once a week from her for something or another, but I wouldn't change her for the world. She keeps us together like the peanut butter on celery.

We pulled up to school and parked our bikes on the rack, "We'll I'll see you at gym class, don't forget we have swimming today. Hope you brought your lunch cause it's mystical Monday and who knows what they be serving today! Chow!"

I swung my rucksack on my shoulder thinking about lunch time; it's scary no matter what school you go to. Thank God I have an iron stomach.

Chapter 2

By the end of the day I was ready to stop and have a cappuccino at our local kaffeehaus- coffee house. We all stopped there everyday after classes to unwind and relax, nothings better than biscotti and cappuccino. We eat late at our house because dad doesn't get home till super late, so I'm usually starving again by then.

We grabbed our favorite table which was outside by the water fountain; it's such a beautiful town full of character and culture. There are flower baskets hanging from all the street lights making it appealing to look at.

It's a small village twenty minutes by train to Munich and everything was within riding or walking distance, I love the way it's laid out its all very quaint. Mom and I come to the Kaffeehaus on the weekend when Dad's gone traveling for work. He goes every month for a few days at a time and travels the globe. Sometimes he's allowed for us to accompany him; we got to go to turkey last year. It's kind of nice when he's gone mom and me have some quality time for just us. Plus mom says it keeps the romance alive between them.

Bam! I got pegged in the face with a spilt ball, "What's up?" I yelled.

"You were looking too serious for our table." Matthias said as he hit me with another one, it smacked me right in between the eyes.

"Paybacks suck you know! You never know when your going to get them" I smiled at him with a smirk.

"Don't make me separate you two again!" Steffi warned us.

"Let's talk about this birthday party. What's left for us to do? Do we need anything else for it? Is everything all in place?" she asked as she pulled out her notebook full of detailed stuff for the party she'd been working on for it.

"Miss ready for action" we teased.

"Decorations? Check. Food and drinks, how's that going?"

"Mom is taking care of all the food and she bought tons of drinks for us. She's making a lot of potato salad, desserts, and fruit and veggie plates. We're gonna grill the sausages on the bonfire as needed."

"I'm bringing my favorite cherry brandy and hobnobs for myself and I might just share with you, it being your birthday and all," Steffi laughed.

"My mom's baking your cake as well, your mom asked her to make the rum cake and carrot cake you love."

"Sweet! I love them."

"I'm also bringing the Ouija board to mess with for when we're inside for the night. Also I have lawn games and other blow up boats and rafts for the pond. We should have plenty to keep us busy, not to mention the bonfire."

"Wunderbar- wonderful!" I cheered.

"Danka, for your help." I gave Steffi a bear hug, she almost fell off her chair, with that she put away her notebook and we relaxed before we had to go to soccer practice.

"We gotta go, we're due in fifteen on the field," I said as I looked at my watch.

"Let's do it." Matthias got up and we headed for the bikes.

After practice I was beat tired and my kaffee buzz was no existing. I said, "Guten Abend-good night" to Matthias and headed for home.

It took the last of my energy to peddle home but when I got there was a heavenly aroma filling the house, lamb kabobs and fresh bread. "Shower, dinners in twenty bitter," Mom said as I slid past her to hang up my stuff.

"WOW! It smells great"

"I wish I could say that about you!" she laughed.

"Hand me your clothes and I'll start them soaking."

Dinner was amazing tasting and it was great having dad home again. We talked all about my birthday party as we ate. We covered the decorations to the rules, which aren't too many, my parents trust me.

They did say that everyone's parents had been notified and informed that we're holding the party at the garden haus and that everyone who wants can stay the night over. Plus they would be driving kids home along with Steffi's mom up unto three am.

After that, they are stuck staying the evening, they said. We all agreed to the rules and with that, it was set. I helped clear the table then went straight up to bed and crashed in ten minutes.

Chapter 3

By the end of the week, everyone that knew me was headed over to our garden haus for the party of the year. We'd set up almost everything the day before so the only things left were the food and drinks.

By five o'clock we were ready to relax and party. Mom and Dad dropped off the last of the supplies; they hugged me and reminded me and Matthias that they'd be back later to take kids home. Steffi told them not to worry that we'd be fine and she'd keep an eye on things.

Soon people started drifting in and the party was a go. Two hours later everyone was having a blast and there was a mountain of gifts piled on the table in the house. At ten pm, my closest friend made a toast to me, "Cheers um ihre gesundheit!-cheers to your health" I was clicking my glass to Steffi when I saw him.

He was dressed just like me, same hair, eyes, he even smiled like me. He walked over to me, stood in front of me, then he tapped my glass to a drink and suddenly disappeared before my eyes. I was left standing there wondering what I have just seen, maybe I've had too much to drink, I thought to myself and I was seeing double and was lightheaded. I shook my head then decided to have a snack to feel better.

I made a plate full of food and sat down by the bonfire where Miriam and Steffi were enjoying fresh strawberries and cherry brandy.

"Hey ladies, are you enjoying the party?"

"Of course we are. We sent Matthias to get wood for the fire a few minutes ago."

"Gotta keep warm," I said.

"So what's happening down by the lake? I haven't gotten there yet but it looks busy," I said as I was watching them.

"Some of the macho men are daring the other guys and girls to go skinny dipping."

"I think we should go steal their clothes while there in the water as a joke." Steffi said with a huge cheesy grin.

"That'd be funny for sure. Good luck with that." I said as I finished up my plate full of food and headed to make rounds. The music was a low rumble and the bonfire was roaring. I'd set hay bails around the fire to sit on and most of them were filled. As I was walking, talking to everyone, one of the girls asked me how I got back from the lake so fast. I didn't have a clue what she was talking about.

"What? I was just sitting at the bonfire having food a minute ago."

"Oh, I swore you were just at the lake with us."

She smiled then walked away. Weird I thought.

That's when I heard the yelling down by the lake. I and a bunch of us ran down there to check what was going on as fast as we could. We got there just as Tomas was pulling Nik out of the water—he was limp and not moving.

"What the hell were you doing Wilhelm?" he stated.

"What are you talking about?" I looked at him puzzled.

"We got him—Nik?Nik? Can you hear me?"

"Turn him over and pat his back," someone said. Within a few seconds he was coughing out water. We all cheered.

"Oh my gosh Nik what happened to you?" I asked.

"Stay away from me Wilhelm, you've done enough!"

"It's your entire fault, you almost drowned me!" I stood there looking at him; I couldn't believe he thought I was capable of doing that to him.

"He was with me at the bonfire Nik, not by here at all." Steffi told him.

He pushed her out of the way as if he didn't believe. Everyone was starring at me. "We saw you Wilhelm, you were in the water dunking him." A few of them said.

"No, I wasn't, I was by the bonfire up by the garden haus, I swear! I don't know what you saw but it wasn't me." I stood there with Matthias starring at the lake trying to figure out what was going on.

I looked at him. "I don't know what I saw but it looked like you, Wil. I believe you tho." We walked back together to the party a few minutes later. Some of the guys left with Nik soon after that.

By fourteen hundred hour the fire and the party wound down. All of the kids left were staying the night with us. We all sat around the last of the glowing embers of the fire as mom and dad took the last car full of the kid's home. They said, "Nacht, ich liebe dich- night, I love you" with a hug and left us.

We were all telling stories about ghost and other creepy things when Steffi and Matthias pulled out the Ouija board. We made a table out of the hay bails to use. There were ten of us there but some of the girls were too afraid to play and one of the couples took off alone to go to the lake.

Everyone positioned themselves around the board as Steffi told us the rules of the game, "We all put one finger on the planchet, no one breaks the circle once we start, we circle around the board once for everyone who's playing and always say goodbye because we don't want any evil spirits lingering here after we're done."

She looked around at everyone, "Ready? Let's play," we all placed a finger on and the planchet and it started to move.

CHAPTER 4

Round and round the planchet went over the board, "Is someone there?" Steffi asked.

"Who's there? Tell us your name?" it suddenly stopped on "K" and kept going. It spells out "Kristoph."

"Who are you Kristoph? How did you die?" it went round and round spelling Kristoph over and over. It started stopping on letters again…

"C-o-r-d, A-r-o-u-n-d, n-e-c-k"

"Awe, that's so sad," Miriam said out loud.

"What do you want with us?" another girl asked him.

"W-i-l-h-e-l-m" it spelled out slowly.

"Ok, who's messing with the game?" I asked. I took my finger off the planchet and smiled.

"Having fun with me?" I asked everyone eyeing them.

"I didn't do it," they all started to say one by one.

"Put your finger back on it."

"Was auch immer- whatever." I said as I placed my finger back on.

"What do you want with Wilhelm?" They asked him.

"L-i-f-e"

"Ok, I'm done playing" I said as I got up and walked away.

"I need a beer and pretzels"

THEY RETURN

Matthias came up to me while I was at the table; "I'm sure they were just having a laugh with you, no worries" He smiled.

"It's getting late, everyone, let's head into the garden haus and lay out our sleeping bags." I said to everyone.

I held the door open for everyone as they carried in their things from the pile of bags by the door. We laid out the sleeping bags and climbed in them. We turned down the lights and told ghosts stories. I was in the middle of my story when I saw a shadow outside the window.

At first I didn't think much of it but then I saw a face lurking at me, staring straight into the haus. It was him again, the guy who looked just like me again, only this time I got a good look at him. He was dressed just like me and stood there looking eye to eye at me.

"What the hell? There's a guy starring in the window looking at us!" I said excitedly.

Everyone looked at me then out the window, "Stop trying to scare us, Wilhelm!" Miriam shouted at me as she took a long drink off her bottle of water.

"I'm not trying to scare you-I know I saw someone looking in at us."

Matthias got up with Tomas and looked out the window, "No ones out there now so, don't worry about it. It's probably just one of your neighbors."

Everyone agreed and we all lay back down.

"I know what I saw, it wasn't a neighbor!"

Steffi looked at me, "Enough ghost stories for one night. Let's try and get some sleep." I said as I turned off the lights as I walked back to my sleeping bag.

"Thank you so much all of you for a great birthday everyone" I fell asleep thinking about the guy I saw wondering if I was just seeing things or was it really someone who looked like me. Within twenty minutes I was out cold snoring.

My sleep was disturbing; I dreamed I was drowning Nik and then the guy who looked like me was trying to choke me; I woke up sweating profusely all over. I tried to go back to sleep but I was still tossing and turning when the sun came up. Morning couldn't have come soon enough; I know I saw something I'm just not sure exactly what It was. I'd know soon enough though.

Chapter 5

By Monday, I thought everyone would be back to normal and not upset anymore, but I was wrong.

Half of the soccer team wasn't talking to me and they were spreading rumors about what I supposedly did at the party. After half a day trying to convince my friends that I didn't do I gave up and decided that they just needed time for it to blow over. At least Matthias and Steffi and a few others believed me and they were saying that I was with them so I couldn't have done what they said I did.

After lunch, outside under the shelter house I got up to dump my tray off when someone ran right into me from behind. I turned around, it was him, the boy who looked just like me, my doppelganger. He was dressed just like me, he looked at me then gave me a crooked smile as he reached out to touch my cheek, and then a second later he disappeared into thin air like he was never there in the first place.

I ran back to Steffi, "Did you see him? He was right behind me! He was just starring at me and reached out and touched my face!"

"Who are you talking about?" She asked me puzzled looking.

"Him, my twin! He looks just like me! Oh man, he was just there then he vanished right in front of me." I bellowed.

"Are you feeling alright?"

"I'm fine; really I swear I just saw him again!"

She shook her head no and then walked away.

"Maybe I'm seeing things after all," I thought out loud. I just don't know what's going on anymore, what in the world is happening?

I was in deep thought when I went back to my locker to grab my books when Matthias came up to me and asked "Why did you ignore me in the lunchroom, you mad at me or something?"

"What? I didn't see you down there and no, I'm not mad at you."

"Alright then, next time don't act like that then."

"Remember when I said I saw somebody that looked like me? Well I saw them again down at lunch today." I said as I cleared my throat waiting for him to say something.

"That's strange did you talk to him?"

"No, he disappeared before I could say anything. I think I'm losing it." I waited for him to tell me I'm not but it never came.

"Well, if you see him again talk to him and ask what he wants." With that he walked off leaving me to contemplate what he just said. I never once thought of asking him that. Next time I'll be more prepared if there is a next time that is.

Later I headed to the bathroom between classes and when I went to wash my hands; I glanced up and that's when I saw him standing behind me in the mirror. "What the heck is going on?" I said as I swung around fast.

"Who are you and what do you want?" I belted.

He just stood there smiling at me and then started to laugh.

"What do you want from me?" I asked again.

"I want to use the bathroom!"

"What? Oh sorry I didn't see you there." I said as he walked into the bathroom.

"You alright?" he asked.

"Yea, I'm fine." When I turned back he was already gone but there was a message in blood on the mirror… "Come play with me!" I stood there with huge eyes in a state; I grabbed my rucksack and ran out of the bathroom as fast as I could. I was shaking by the time I got to class. I was freaked out the rest of the day.

Chapter 6

I biked alone after school, I needed time to think; by the time I got to the Kaffee haus I was feeling a little better. Steffi and Miriam were already there. Matthias was sitting with Nik when I walked in.

I grabbed a drink and walked to the table where the girls were. Steffi could tell I wasn't my normal self and asked, "You doing alright? You look upset." She leaned into me, and then smiled.

"Just having a rough day today that's all."

"Matthias told us about lunch today. Wanna talk about it?" Miriam asked.

Everyone at the table looked at me until I answered.

"Do you believe in doppelgangers?"

"You mean a twin? Then yes I believe it's possible," She said.

"Me too, I believe it as well." Miriam chimed in.

"What's this all about?"

I took a deep breath and then said, "Ever since the party, I've been seeing my twin all over the place. I have seen him twice today alone. I think he was the one who tried to drown Nik in the lake. I saw him in the bathroom, he was standing right behind me but then when I turned he was gone, and there was a message written on the mirror then he vanished into thin air again. I asked him what he wanted but he only laughed."

"What did the message say?" they all were looking at me.

"Come play with me! it was written in blood" I shuddered at the thought of it again.

"That's creepy!" Steffi said. I agreed it was.

"Well you know what they say about doppelgangers-they only show up when they want to take over your life. Their evil."

"Really, Miriam? I'm sure it's all made up, no one wants to hurt you Wilhelm." Steffi said, trying to calm down the situation.

"I'm sure there are other reasons."

"Yea, maybe" I mumbled.

After that I headed home. Mom and dad were surprised to see me so early.

"What are you doing home so early, Wilhelm?" Mom inquired.

"I thought you went with some of the team to the park,"

"No, I was at the Kaffee haus with my friends."

"We just saw you ten minutes ago." Dad said.

I looked at them taking in what they said, "Oh, well I changed my mind"

I lied, no reason to freak them out. They obviously saw him too.

"Well it's going to be two hours before dinner so if you want to go back to the park you can." Mom smiled at me.

I thought it over then decided that maybe I should go check it out. Who knows what he might do. I needed to check it out for myself.

When I got to the park, I spotted the guys. They were practicing passing the ball around. I watched for a few minutes as they kicked it back and forth. That's when I spotted him, he was running with the ball forward toward the goal and then he suddenly saw me. He spotted me stopped running then flashed a wicked grin then kicked the ball toward the street instead of the goal. Tomas ran after it without looking, heading straight toward an oncoming car that he didn't see.

The car hit him hard and he went flying through the air like a rag doll, all I could do is watch the horror of it all. He hit the pavement with such force we heard it as he bounced off it. He just laid there not moving.

"Oh my God! Tomas! Tomas! Can you hear me?" I yelled as I ran toward him. The man in the car raced out and tried to help him.

"Don't move him—I'm calling the medics" he yelled.

We all stood around hoping he'd wake up but he never did. I looked over at the park, my twin was standing there waving at me then in a flash, he was gone. The medics showed up, assisted Tomas, loaded him up and headed for the hospital.

After that everyone was blaming me because I kicked the ball into the street.

"What's wrong with you lately? First Nik now Tomas! You want someone to die?" they shouted.

Great, they all think I'm trying to pick off all my friends. Now what do I do? I wondered. After a minute they all turned their backs on me and walked away, leaving me there alone feeling ashamed and hurt not to mention scared cause my twin was causing havoc wherever he went. It will only get worse I thought. I have to stop him before he does kill someone or me.

Chapter 7

I stumbled in the door of my house a few minutes later. Mom met me at the door, "I heard what happened at the park, Nik's mom called me a minute ago. What were you thinking? Why didn't you warn him? Nik's mom said you caused the accident. Is that true?" she stared at me with intense eyes.

"Mom you don't understand! Someone else is doing those things, not me! I can't explain what's happening but it's not me!" I shouted.

Dad came running in the room, "Oh, your homes… were very upset with you! I can't believe you would do this to Tomas or Nik."

"I didn't." I insisted but they weren't about to listen to me.

"Go to your room, well deal with this later when were calm." Dad shouted.

I walked to my room defeated, holding my head down. Now even my parents were against me. I had to find out what was going on before anything else happened. I thought about it all night long.

By morning, I had conceived a plan, this all started when we played with the Ouija board so I'd start there. The next day I went to school and told Matthias what happened but he already heard. He still believed my innocents so at least I had some allies on my side still. We conjured up a plan to meet after school at the garden haus and stay the night. Hopefully mom and dad would agree. We'd discuss this, then we get there, we agreed.

I raced home after school and asked my parents if I could go. Luckily they were in better moods and said yes. Mom packed me some snacks and drinks to take and then I headed out to pick up Matthias on the way. He'd invited Miriam and Steffi to go as well.

Fifteen minutes later, we arrived there. Within the hour, the girls were there too, we discussed the plan and started it in motion. We put the food away, and then took out the game where it all started; we had to get to the bottom of this once and for all.

Steffi put candles around us as well as a salt circle, for our protection she informed us. We sat down inside the circle, lit the candles, placed our fingers on the planchet and were ready to make contact.

We circled the board once for each of us then Steffi called out, "We're trying to make contact with the twin Kristophare, you here?" At first, nothing happened then the planchet started moving with incredible speed around the board then it went to the top of the board.

"Yes," it said.

"Is that you Kristoph?"

Yes again.

"Why are you here? What do you want with Wilhelm?"

The planchet moved, "L-i-f-e."

"What is it that you want with my life?" I asked.

It spelled out "Mine."

"What do you mean?"

"I-t-s m-i-n-e," it spelled out.

"How is it yours? And why are you after me?" I huffed feeling anxious.

Suddenly the board started to shake, it started bouncing up and down just then the planchet flew off the board went flying toward the window and shattered it; that's when we noticed Kristoph standing there looking in at us.

He stared at us coldly, flashed a smile.

"Do you all see him?" I asked.

Everyone nodded but then in a split second he was gone again. I grabbed the planchet and the board, we placed our fingers quickly back on it. It went round and round "m-y l-i-f-e, m-y- t-w-i-n," it spelled.

We all looked at each other then suddenly there was a gust of wind coming through the room, the candles all went out, then within a second they all lit back up! That's when the board flew out of the circle and landed right behind me.

We all sat there frozen scared not knowing what to do afraid to move, "I think that's enough for tonight, don't you?"

We all nodded in a daze, shocked by what just happened.

At least we got a little information but not enough to help sadly.

Chapter 8

The next morning, everyone went home after breakfast quickly, everyone was still a little freaked out about yesterday's happenings. I stayed behind thinking about it all, running it though my head again and again. Not only was I worried, now I was truly frightened as well and I hadn't a clue as to what to do to fix the situation.

All I knew was that my twin was growing stronger and stronger with each passing day and I was in direr straights with worry. I had to come up with an idea that would disintegrate the situation and put everything back as it was.

This twin of mine had to go back to where he came from, he didn't belong here weather he thought so or not. While I was brainstorming, I decided to ask mom if I was really a twin or was this just some demon trying to trick me? What else was I to think? If I was she could tell me what happened, it was my only option.

Now I have to come up with a way to inquire about it without being to abrupt. I'd ask her tonight, hopefully I'll get something useful to use against him.

Dinner was the perfect time to talk; dad was out of town again so I'd be just the two of us. Dinner was late and there was a lot of small talk between us. I think mom knew something was up. By dessert I had enough courage to ask her, "Mom, was I always an only child? Was there ever a twin or someone?"

She literally choked on her wine. "Why would you ask me that, Wilhelm? Who have you been talking to?" she had a worried look in her eye.

"No one mom I swear, I was just wondering because I always thought it would be great to have a twin," I smiled as I went back to eating my pie.

"Wilhelm," she was choked up but trying to talk. There were tears in her eyes as she looked at me.

"Yes Wilhelm, you were a twin" She said quietly.

"What happened to him?"

She cleared her throat and said, "He died at birth, the cord wrapped around his neck and he was breach. By the time he came out he was blue and not breathing."

I stared at her, "How terrible that must have been for you, Oh mom, I'm so sorry."

I wrapped my arms around her and held her as she started to cry.

"They tried to bring him back but it was too late. He was unconscious for too long. He was much smaller and weaker than you and just didn't survive." She was sobbing now.

I just held her not knowing what to say, "Its ok mom, you still have me." I mumbled.

"I know you're my everything Wilhelm, I love you so much."

"I love you too mom."

Later that night as I lay in bed I heard laughter coming from the other room. Mom had cried herself to sleep so I knew it wasn't her. I thought maybe it was the radio or the TV left on so I went out to turn it off.

I walked out and headed for the family room. It was pitch black so I headed toward the kitchen; I thought I heard something rattle in there. I opened the door and walked in. I turned on the light and there was blood all over the place, on the walls, the counters, on the floor. On top of the table was my cat ripped open like he had surgery on him. It was a gruesome site, I gagged as I looked.

THEY RETURN

The table was dipping blood onto the floor and there was a message written in blood, "Your next!" I stood there trying to take it all in—I looked out of the corner of my eye and saw my twin standing there with a knife in his hand.

He was waving it back and forth, laughing then without warning he threw the knife at me, I ducked just in the nick of time and it went flying behind me; it stuck deep into the wall. He had a maniacal look in his eyes and then he disappeared leaving me standing there in the middle of chaos. I stood there in daze then I hit me, I ran to the trash can and threw up. It was all just too much for me. After a minute I got my head on right and knew I was the one who had to clean this mess up before mom saw it.

Thank goodness it was the middle of the night; it took me hours to clean up all the blood and guts. By the time I got done it was early in the morning. What a horrible mess it was, I didn't know what to do with the cat, it was mom's baby. She was going to be heartbroken when she found out.

I put it in a large trash bag under my bed until I could dispose of it properly. I decided I would tell her it ran out the door when I went off to school and thought I'd come back when ready. I tried to lie down and go back to sleep but it never came. I was creeped out and it's hard to sleep knowing you have a dead pet under your bed.

Finally my alarm went off and I stumbled out of bed. I put the cat in my rucksack, I'd take and bury it in the garden haus later. I avoided mom and took off for school.

Chapter 9

At school, I was preoccupied by the terrible night I had to endure. Over lunch time I explained what happened last night but spare Steffi, she loved the cat too much to hear about its operation.

Matthias was shocked by it all. "How's he getting stronger? What can we do to help you stop him?" he asked.

All good questions I thought, "Ever since the party and that damn board game!" I slammed my fist down on the table.

Steffi came running over.

"What's wrong? Are you leaving me out again for a reason?" she questioned me.

"No, but it was so revolting that I didn't want you to have to deal with it, that's all."

"What did I miss?"

I went through it again deleting some of the gruesome details and by the time I was done we were all worried and shocked. After a few beats Steffi said, "You know, I've been thinking about it and I think he's coming after us because we didn't say goodbye when we played on the board. Now he has freedom to roam and we can't stop him." She looked seriously at us.

"But, there's got to be away."

THEY RETURN

By the end of the day, we headed toward the kaffee haus to try and figure out a plan of attack to banish the twin for good. We talked for an hour and were still empty handed. How do you get rid of a ghost like present before it's too late? I wondered. I excused myself from the table to go to the bathroom and when I came back, he was sitting there at the table taking to Steffi! As soon as he saw me he disappeared.

I ran to the table, "You were just talking to him! What did you say?"

"What? That wasn't you? She looked around.

"Really? He looked and acted just like you."

"It was him! Oh my gosh, he's getting bolder. He told me he wanted to take over my life the other day; I think he's doing a good job of it." I sat down.

"Yeah, he's just like you!"

We finished our kaffees and left, I headed straight home. I was worried about mom. When I got there she was out back sitting with her friend talking, "Hi mom, I'm home now."

"Of course you are, you've been home. You just brought us tea ten minutes ago silly." She smiled and shook her head.

"Oh yeah, I was just messing around." I told her with a smile,

"Do you need anything?"

"No, we're good. Thank you." I shut the door and went in.

"I know you're here, where are you?" I shouted.

"Come out where I can see you!" I found him in my room; he was standing there looking in a mirror at himself. He stared at me as I walked closer to him, "Was willst du? - what do you want?"

"Dein leben! Your life!" he hissed.

"I want your life Wilhelm, you've had it for eighteen years, and now it's my turn."

He went back to looking in the mirror again.

"You can't have it! It's mine."

"You opened the door and now you're going to pay for it. It's your fault; you murdered me in the womb. I was supposed to be your equal." He explained.

"It's not my fault it, I was a baby!" I yelled at him.

"Soon it will be mine turn for good." And with that he disappeared. I stood there in disbelief.

"I'm running out of time." I said out loud.

"Come help me cook Wilhelm, I love it when we cook together." Mom yelled to me.

"Sure mom, be there in a minute." I tried to put what happened behind me until later.

"Mom, what are we making tonight?"

"Your dad's favorite, beef burgundy and homemade fresh bread. We'll start the bread first so it can rise while we make the sauce."

After half an hour the bread was ready for the oven and the house was starting to smell wonderful. Before long everything was ready and we kept it in the oven to stay warm until dad was due home. Mom gave me a hug and said, "Women love a man that can cook, I'm so proud of you."

We went into the family room and put on a movie while we waited for dad to get home after we cleaned up the kitchen. He arrived an hour later. We ate then mom and him headed to the back deck to sit and talk. I grabbed a bottle of their favorite wine and took it out to them. I sat for a few minutes filling him in on what he missed while he was gone.

"We would have won our game if Nik would have blocked the final shot, he let it go."

"You'll stop them next time," Dad is always the optimist.

"Danka for dinner, it was wunderbar! I'll clean up while you two talk then I'm going to bed. Guten abend- good night." I grabbed the dishes off the table and went to the kitchen to wash them and put them away. I grabbed the dessert and cut two pieces then took them out, "Glad you're home, dad. Love you mom, enjoy your talk."

"Night Wilhelm."

Chapter 10

I brushed my teeth then hopped into bed; I wasn't tired so I decided to read. I'd gotten a book on possession from the library so I read some of it; maybe it would lead me in the right direction.

By thirteen hundred hours, I had finished it. I sat there in a daze thinking about its content. I closed my eyes to relax and fell into a deep sleep.

The air felt heavy. I could smell the musty old scent of the ripened earth and there were darkened shadows all around, as I walked aimlessly through the forest of trees.

The branches reached out grabbing my shirt and pants as the night creatures sung an eerie melody as I slowly moved through them. I saw a presents move closer to me, then I heard my name being called as if it were carried on the wind…

"Wilhelm come to me," it cut through the air like razors.

I walked without fear; it was if the voice was controlling me now, pulling me in further. The closer I got to the shadow it came into view, it was Kristoph. He was dressed just like me in a pair of jeans and a striped shirt standing there watching me. We stood there for a minute staring at each other then he held out his hand; I grabbed it as he pulled me closer into him.

He spoke in a soft manner that was calming, "Komm zu mir- come to me, we can be one, let us be together again."

I looked him in his eyes, I was drawn in deeper and deeper, I couldn't move.

"Let us be forever together," he said to me.

He opened his mouth and a black mist came out of it – the mist poured into my mouth, I started to chock as it filled my lungs. My head spun like it was inside a tornado and my eyes went blurry as I fell to my knees coughing.

Gagging for air I woke up coughing trying to catch my breath. Kristoph was standing beside me looking at me, He reached out and touched my face, then all was calm.

"Jetxt stehen wire in-stand now we are one" I stood up slowly taking his hand, everything came into focus, I felt different, stronger, more complete, more alive than ever I had been. I could hear Kristoph's voice in my head now, it was calming and soothing, and it faded into mine.

He smiled at me as I smiled back at him and said, "Yes, we are one now forever." I stood up next to him standing side by side, "Yes, we are one now. We'll be together forever." I repeated to him.

Holding hands we walked together into our parents' room united as one now and forever.

    As an avid bookworm and writer, I like nothing better than curling up with my cats and reading or writing a new book. I'm also a mother of four incredible kids that rock my world. I'm an outdoor enthusiast who loves to boat all day, sleep out under the stars and tell ghost stories around the bonfire all night. I enjoy working at a haunted house where I act, help with costumes and do fx make-up on my twisted family of ghouls.

AUTHOR'S NOTE

I've always been attracted to the grotesque world of people with questionable morals, the people that should have a warning label on them. I'm addicted. I can't stop myself and apparently neither can you. After researching enough women who do/did the unthinkable to other people, I realize that women who kill are truly rare and unfamiliar to our society. Women are usually viewed as nurturers and most people have a hard time believing that a woman of all people could become so violent as to become a serial killer. Women aren't usually viewed as being homicidal, making it that much harder to convict a woman than it is a male. The average male serial killer murders 4.2 years before being caught, whereas females on the other hand average 8.4 years, causing more crimes in those extra years they weren't caught. Women also tend to financially benefit from their crimes and have a strong relationship with their victims as well. Usually they are the last person on earth who you'd think would have committed the crime to begin with. With all that said, go on and read this book. I dare you but once you read it, you can never unread it and some of it will truly haunt your mind. Welcome to my world.

LULU OF THE RED MARKET

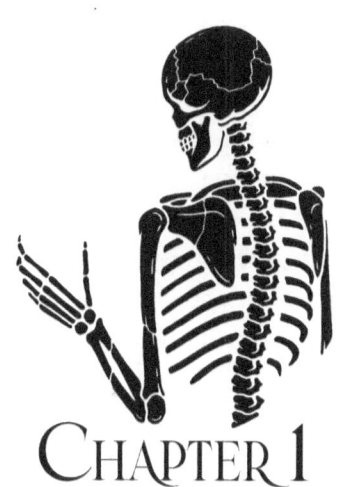

Chapter 1

"Push! Push! You can do it—breathe and on the next contraction push hard, we're almost there. Doing good I can see the head. Push! Damn… the cords wrapped around the neck. I don't know if I can get it, the baby's airs cut off. Damn! Push, we're losing her, you have to push."

"No! My baby!" Minutes were ticking away and the baby wasn't moving. "I'm going to pull on the next contraction, ready? Now push!" The baby was out but she wasn't breathing and was blue. "Start the compressions, let's get her back… mom's crashing too—were losing them both…"

***

I woke to my ferret, Little Cobb, licking my nose to wake me up. He always does this when he hears my alarm going off for school. He and my cat, Zeba, usually end up in my bed sometime during the night. I'm single, so they take over the other side of the bed.

I grabbed Little Cobb and kissed his ear then put him next to me, he ran down the stairs that I built for him to be able to get up on and down on the bed; he looked like a slinky as he tumbled down them. Both he and the cat run to the kitchen every morning, like they're starving 'cause they know it's breakfast time. I finished getting dressed and headed downstairs.

My name is Rainey and I'm a health teacher at Wallace High School. I've been teaching for several years and I have gone through several different grades but after teaching at the high school level I've finally realized I enjoy it the best.

I love my students, they always keep me on my toes, you never know what's gonna come out of their mouths. For the last few months my health class has been collecting soda cans along with my neighbors, and this month we finally had enough money to order a new skeleton for the health room; it was to be the pride and joy of the room. Today I would share the good news with the students, they were sure to be as excited; it would show them how when we all work together we can accomplish something.

I had got up early this morning so I could enjoy my breakfast. It was only six-thirty so I had plenty of time. I made eggs and toast with peach jam on it, my favorite. Also, I made a large pot of coffee to go with it. I was sitting at my table looking through my catalog of health stuff I'd like to have for my room while I ate. I had cut out the picture of the skeleton months ago and hung it on my fridge. I had also made a full size skeleton for my room out of paper and hung it up on the bulletin board. We colored it in as we got closer to the goal.

I'd be placing the order sometime today for the skeleton. It would be coming from India; it's one of the only places to get a full one. They actually have a market there called "The Red Market" where you can get paid to sell your body parts. Most of the kidneys donated come from there for transplant.

Half of the population in India has donated one kidney, but you get more money for your skeleton. It will be great having a model for when I talk about bones.

I finished up my toast and eggs, threw my plate in the dishwasher and loaded my thermos for school. I always had coffee; it keeps me going all day.

Today's flavor was pumpkin spice; I filled up my thermos and headed out the door. It was a beautiful fall day, the sun was shining and the trees looked like they were on fire with the sunlight shining through them. I walked over to the flower garden on my way to the car and picked a few stems of flowers for my classroom then I headed to work.

I got there a little earlier than normal; I filled up my vase with water and sat the flowers on my desk. Then I made a sign saying we'd finally earned enough to order the skeleton and colored in the rest of the skeleton on the board. First bell rang, slowly the class started trickling in; by the last bell the rest ran in.

"Quiet everyone! I have an announcement… we finally earned enough to order the skeleton! I'll be placing the order today."

Everyone cheered and clapped.

"Good job on helping save the money, without your help we would have not been able to do it." I smiled at everyone.

"We're also going to study the heart today and Friday we will have a quiz."

So much for the students being happy campers, now everyone booed.

"The quiz will have bonus questions on it about random bone names, so look over the chart in your book."

The rest of the day went smoothly and finally the end of the day came. I waved goodbye to all the kids, gathered my things and headed downstairs, I had to make copies of the test paper before tomorrow so I went to the teachers' lounge and placed the quiz on the copier and hit start. As the pages copied I thought about the skeleton. I hoped it would have all of its teeth; I had a thing about teeth, I'm sure it will be beautiful.

The paper tests were almost done copying when the art teacher, Jet, walked in. "Hey there! How goes it today with everything?"

I said, "Just fine, we finally saved enough money to order our skeleton for our room. I'm ordering it today."

She smiled and said, "Yeah, I heard some of the kids talking about it."

"I'm almost done with the copier. You need it too? What's the new project this week?" She held up a page full of different styles of Moroccan lanterns made out of paper. There were some really pretty ones.

"Wow! I love them! You can make me one for my house if you want. I love the colors orange and red."

"No problem, I can do that so my students see how we make one step by step."

I gathered my papers and let her make copies. I said goodbye and left to go home. I was almost home when I forgot I had to stop at the grocery store for the basics, have to have my coffee and milk. I turned the car around and headed to Whole Foods.

This was going to be a record breaker, I always time myself in the store, it helps me from over buying. It was four o'clock, I headed in, grabbed a cart and was off. I went down a few of the food isles gathering drinks, tuna, sushi, cat food, milk and coffee. I can't forget the coffee I'd be lost without it, I grabbed several different kinds. I think half of my food bill is coffee.

I went to the self check out and proceeded to check out. I grabbed my change and left. Twenty-two minutes! I made great time.

Now, it's time to head home and relax. I don't have any school papers to grade tonight so I had the whole night to myself, just me, my cat, and my ferret. I had been thinking about asking one of my guy friends, Charlie, to come for dinner and a movie, but I still was debating. I pulled into the driveway and started carrying the bags in. Jerry, my next door neighbor was cutting his grass again; I call him the, "Lawn Nazi" because he cuts his grass every day.

The air smelled of fresh cut grass, I waved hello to him and headed inside with my bags.

I placed the bags on the counter then headed to get a wine glass; I was a wine enthusiast and was a member of the wine of the month club. This month's wine was Moscato, a sweet white wine.

It is one of my favorite flavors so far. The Riesling, another flavor of wine, was also a nice smooth flavor. I took a long drink from the glass; it was a good start to my evening. I decided that I would invite Charlie over for dinner. I have plenty of everything and company's always nice. I grabbed the phone and called him, he was happy to come. He said it would be about a half hour before he could get there.

"No problem, get here when you can and I'll see you soon." I hung up, finished my glass of wine and headed upstairs to change into something more comfortable.

After that, I headed back to the kitchen, put everything away and got out the appetizers and sushi. I arranged them on a glass serving tray, then took out another wine glass and headed to the living room with the tray of food. I grabbed the phone to place the ordered for our skeleton. It was hard to understand them on the line due to their accent. They said it would be a few weeks and gave me a confirmation number. I couldn't wait to see it.

I had just finished my second glass of wine and some cheese and crackers when Charlie got there.

"Well, hello there stranger! Glad you could come I've missed you." I said as I opened the door and he walked in.

"Always glad to see you too," he said as he gave my cheek a kiss.

Charlie and I have been friends since grade school. We'd been there for each other for the ups and the downs of life. He's my best friend and I just love him to death.

"I got sushi, and crackers to go with your favorite, cheese, the goat cheese you always go on about and wine. Can never have too much of a good thing." I winked at him as I sat down next to him on the couch.

I poured him a glass of wine then I held up my wine glass to toast him, "To our friendship, may we always have it."

We clicked our glasses together and took a drink.

"Mmm... This is a great wine, what one is this?" he asked.

"This one is Moscato tonight," he took another drink then grabbed some cheese.

"We always eat so healthy here; I need to do this more at home." He said as he took a bite of the cheese.

"So what's new with you? Are you still researching for your book?" I asked him.

Charlie worked construction but he was a nerd at heart he loved writing and researching things.

"Yeah, I'm still researching. I had to go to downtown library to find some old articles; they didn't have much at our branch."

Charlie had been researching for a book he was writing. This time it was to be a fact book. Anything and everything you could think of was going to be covered. One thing for sure, Charlie was thorough.

"Oh, I got that book of facts about the history of women's health for you. The one I told you about."

I got up to get it off the bookshelf. "Thanks, I've been looking forward to reading it. I've always wondered what women did in the olden days. Should be a great read."

I smiled and added, "I sure enjoyed it. It's scary some of the things they did." We talked awhile about some of the subjects in the book then I served the sushi and some fruit. I told him about reaching our goal and ordering the skeleton. He was happy for me. After we ate, it was getting late so I bid farewell to him and promised we'd do it again soon.

I cleaned up the dinner plates and the leftover things. There was only one cracker left so I ate it; it was a lonely cracker hanging out by itself anyway, right?

I finished my drink, the last of the wine, grabbed a book from the bookshelf and headed upstairs to bed. I usually read for at least an hour before I go to sleep. Tonight's book was a ghost story; I love ghost and vampire stories. I've always been fascinated with them. This ghost story is about Rose Hall of Jamaica, it's one of the most haunted places in Jamaica.

I got my pajamas on, brushed my teeth and hopped into bed. My cat Zeba joined me. She always lies on my extra pillow by my head. After reading for an hour and a half, I was ready to sleep. I kissed Zeba on the head and turned out the light.

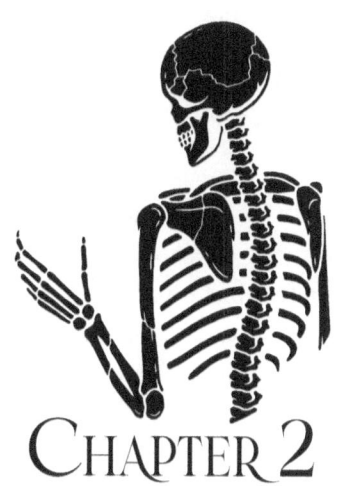

CHAPTER 2

I woke to the chiming of church bells today. Everyday I set a new alarm chime it keeps it interesting; I constantly need change in my life. The bells were comforting, they reminded me of my growing up in Toledo, there was a church close by and I could always hear the bells. I could never tell my parents. I didn't know what time it was because the bells chimed every hour, no being late in our house.

Zeba lifted her head and bonked me it's her way of saying good morning. "Ready, for a new day old girl? Let's go get some coffee and feed you and Little Cobb."

I dressed in my favorite sweater and skirt then headed downstairs. My coffee was already brewing thanks to the new coffee pot Mom got me; it had a timer on it so you can get it going before you get there and I loved it. I poured myself a cup then I got out the raspberry jam and a croissant for breakfast. I wasn't all that hungry probably because I ate so much rice last night. I just sat down to eat and look over my newspaper, when Zeba jumped on the table, "Opps... I forgot your breakfast huh?"

I got up and filled her bowl and gave her a piece of cheese to say I was sorry for forgetting. Just as I was finishing up my ferret ran to the food bowl. I picked him up gave him a kiss on his little ear then let him eat. I had about fifteen minutes before I needed to leave, so I took out the crock pot and started filling it with vegetables and fish that way it would be done when I got home. I added some herbs and put the lid on then grabbed my windbreaker and headed to school.

***

I set my bag down on the desk and turned the lights on. My flowers still looked healthy and smelled wonderful. I loved having plants in my room, made it feel more like a home away from home. I had several plants around the room. I grabbed my watering can and started filling it up. I usually had the students take care of the plants but I felt like doing it today.

My hibiscus tree had grown so big it took up a whole corner and it always had blooms on it. The fichus tree dropped a million leaves a day and drove me nuts but I couldn't abandon it now that I'd had it too long. I had geraniums hanging along the windows. They smelled great and got enough light to produce flowers year round. I had almost finished watering the plants when the last bell rang and someone tapped me on the shoulder, "Do you want me to finish watering?"

It was one of my favorite students, Micah. "No, I'm just about done but thank you." I finished and went to my desk.

"Well, I ordered our skeleton yesterday. It should be here before Halloween. I think the timing's very fitting."

I looked around then said, "Anyone does anything exciting last night? I had dinner with a hottie and pigged out on sushi—can anyone beat that?"

I smiled as I looked around. Then Chad, one of the football players who was a huge brick house raised his hand and said, "I can beat that—I went mud bogging out by the quarry and almost went over the edge! I SAW MY LIFE FLASH BEFORE ME! It didn't take very long."

Everyone was staring at him.

"Well, that sounds fun in a—I don't care if I die kind of way, but defiantly an adrenaline rush. I think you win with your night, I'll try again tonight to top that."

I walked through the room handing out the test papers.

"As you can see we are going to have a pre test to see how much you remember, this one doesn't count unless you do better on it then you do on Fridays test. Any questions before we begin?"

No one raised their hand so I said, "Ok, you can start. good luck, use your little brains for good."

I sat down and started rearranging my desk again; I do it often so it doesn't look like my mom's table. She can't even see the table anymore because it's covered in papers. I looked through all my papers that were in stacks, they were organized in my style of cleaning but a mess to others. After that I went through a bunch of lost and found thing. I made a pile of things kids forgot on the small table that I had candy on it. I put a sign that said, "take me" just like the one out of Alice in Wonderland.

Then I filled up the candy bowl with sweethearts, sixlets, smarties and sour patch kids. I grabbed the bowl then handed out the candy as the kids took their test. After a few minutes most everyone was done.

"Anyone still working?" no one said anything.

"Ok, you can talk the rest of the hour."

The bell rang a few minutes after that and everyone filed out. I grabbed the test and put them on my desk. I'd grade them later today.

It was lunch time, so I grabbed my lunch and then I stopped in the art room and grabbed Jet. We headed to the facility break room; it was the one place no kids were allowed, teacher's solitude. The gym teacher and the band teacher were sitting together debating, everyday it's something new.

"Whatcha boys debating today?" I asked as we took our seats.

"Whether it is better to wear cotton long johns or silk long johns, both have advantages to them. Any comments?"

They both looked up at me and I said, "I prefer silk, I like the way they slide around under your clothes, unlike how cotton sticks."

They smiled then went back to their debate. After a few minutes, the principal, Mr. Wolff came in. At six four and three hundred pounds he was like a moving wall. He was a good man with a kind heart and loved his job even though he had to deal with a lot of the troubled kids. He says that's what drew him to working with kids, so he could help the misunderstood. I agreed with him on how he looked at the troubled ones and I always try to see their point of view and work with them.

"Good afternoon to you all, what's for lunch?" he asked.

I looked up and then said, "It's Taco Tuesday, remember?"

"Oh, yes I do recall that. Hope that lunch is still hot, I'm running late," and he left to go to the lunch line.

Jet and I sat talking about all sorts of different things. The bell was ringing right as I was taking my last bite of apple.

"Well, back to the grind." I said as we walked back to class.

The rest of the day flew by and it was mostly enjoyable. One of my students had a birthday so she brought in cupcakes to share with all of the class. It was the perfect dessert for after lunch. They were carrot cake and chocolate, it was a great combination. We finished up early so I told everyone it was free time; I kept games in my room for such occasions. A few of the kids enjoyed maccala and cards.

I was talking with Joel, about my book I was reading as we finished up the cupcakes. He said he had read the same book and thought it was one of the better written historical ghost story books.

He recommended a few other books as well to me. The bell rang and it was finally the end of the day. I said goodbye to all the students then turned out the lights in the room then walked to my car. The wind was howling so it felt a little colder than it did earlier, at least the sun was still shining. I didn't have any errands to run today so I went straight home.

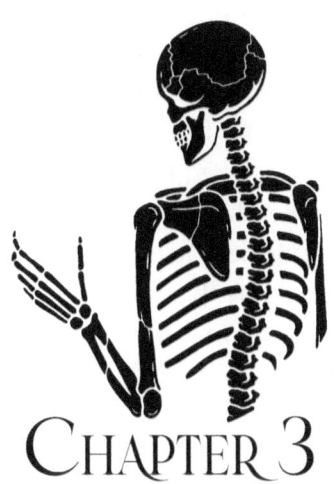

Chapter 3

When I opened the door to the house the smell was heavenly, I couldn't wait to taste dinner. I saw my ferret getting a drink at their food bowl so I picked him up and gave him a kiss on his ear; he rolled over so I could rub his tummy as he chirped at me. He's just the cutest little thing. I gave him a carrot from the fridge and then put him down; he carried it to his lair under the couch. He collected all sorts of things he found interesting, shoes, pizza crust out of the trash, slippers, keys, toilet paper, and a small china kid was probably under there. You name it if it went missing, always checks the lair.

I kicked off my heels, I think a sadistic man made them; the cute shoes are never comfortable or made for walking. I poured myself a glass of wine and went to the family room. I decided that I was going to watch a movie tonight. I grabbed the videos I got from the video store the other day and looked through the pile. I put the movie in the DVD player then went upstairs to change into my pjs and came back down; the movie was ready to watch.

It was Friday night so I planned on staying up late and chilling out. Just as I was about to hit start on the movie, someone knocked on the door. I got up to open the door, it was Charlie.

"Hey, why are you in your pjs already? Am I interrupting?" I smiled at him as he walked in.

"Of course not I was just getting ready to watch a movie and pig out. Want to join me?" he sat down on the couch and chilled.

"I'll get us some drinks. I made dinner too if you want some."

"Oh, yeah is that what I smell? It smells great!" I went to the kitchen and made up two plates. It really did smell wonderful.

I grabbed napkins and headed back to the family room. We got situated and started the movie. Charlie took off his shoes then put them in my lap as he relaxed while the movie started. We were watching a horror movie which is our favorite.

We both liked to comment on the movie as it plays, thank goodness we both do it otherwise we'd drive each other nuts. "Mmm… the food is great. I Love what you did with the fish. You're going to have to come to my house and I'll make you my specialty, rosemary lamb and Caesar salad." We ate as we watched the movie, commenting all the way through.

After the movie was over, Charlie said he was getting up early to go to the library branch in the town next to ours tomorrow. So he kissed my cheek and headed out. I cleaned up and called for my cat. I was going to give her a little of the fish that was left. She came running from upstairs, and followed me to the kitchen when I placed it in her food bowl. The ferret came running into the kitchen five minutes later. I picked him up and gave him a piece of the bread and put him down. He carried it to the food bowl and ate next to Zeba.

A few minutes later, everything was cleaned up so I headed to bed to read. I jumped into bed after I brushed my teeth and started reading. Before I knew it, I had read for two hours. It was two in the morning so I turned off the light and shut my eyes. I was almost asleep when the ferret jumped on my head and woke me up, Zeba jumped on the bed chasing the ferret.

"Guys, I'm trying to sleep!" I yelled at them then I got up and shut my door with the two of them on the other side, and went back to Lala land

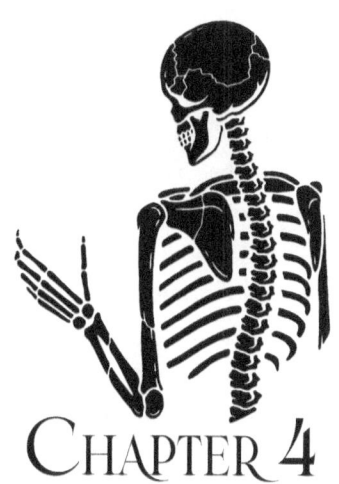

Chapter 4

The weeks flew by and finally one day after school I was grading the student's paper to catch up, and there was a knock on my classroom door. I looked up it was the UPS delivery man.

"Special delivery for Rainey," I smiled and got up.

"That's me."

He carried it in, "It's a little heavy for you probably, so where do you want it? Glad I made it before you left for the night." He said as I pointed to my desk.

He laid it down then held out a clip board for me to sign, "All yours now, have a nice night," and he left.

I was so excited, I started to unwrap it, there were several layers of bubble wrap and I got more excited with each layer. Finally I was staring at a skeleton, it was beautiful. I admired it as I looked it over, it had all of its teeth. I was thrilled. I noticed there was a tag on it, it read—"Lulu had donated her body for you so you could learn from it. Please handle her body with care. Enjoy your new addition."

There was a picture of her on the card holding a baby; I studied it for a few minutes. She looked beautiful; it looked like the two of them were sleeping peacefully.

I said, "Thank you Lulu, for donating your body for my students' sake of knowledge."

I put the stand together and hung Lulu up on it. She was wonderful, the kids will be so surprised tomorrow. I finished grading the last of my papers and placed a sign in Lulu's hand.

It said, "Hello, my name is Lulu."

I placed her hand up like she was waving then I rolled her next to my desk, took one more look at her, and then I turned out the light and headed home.

I was so excited I called Charlie on the drive home. He was happy for me. I asked him how his research was going, we talked for a few minutes then I hung up. I was almost home; when I was craving ice cream so I swung through the drive thru at Cone Palace, the ice cream place by us and got a banana split.

The Lawn Nazi was mowing his grass again when I got home; I waved to him then went inside. I carried in my things in and dropped them on the table then sat down to eat my banana split, it was heavenly. I noticed how nice it was outside while I was eating so I went outside and worked on the yard.

I had spent most of the summer building a rock wall around the yard, I got halfway. I finished the garden area and I've had a lot of compliments on it. Plus I got killer arm muscles now, very defined. I went to the garden and picked out a few rocks to carry over to the end of the wall, I ended up working for a few hours on it.

By the time I got tried it was getting dark and I was starving. I headed in and made peanut butter and jelly sandwiches with raspberry jam. Zeba jumped on my lap hoping for a piece. It's amazing how she and the ferret always know when I'm eating. Five seconds later the ferret came running around the corner. I waited till he was close; then I scooped him up and kissed him. I had saved a little piece of crust for him. It was getting late so I headed upstairs and showered then got into my pjs. By the time I was cleaned up I was worn out so I hit the bed to read.

The light was still on when my alarm went off in the morning. Another new day in paradise, I needed coffee and peeps. I hurried, got dressed then headed downstairs; the coffee smell hit me mid stairs. Zeba and the stinky slinky almost knocked me over on the way down, apparently they were hungry too. I think they're just stomachs on legs.

I hurried, ate and left for school, I wanted to be there before any of the students saw Lulu. I made great time going across town, parked and went in.

I unlocked my room, turned on the lights, Lulu wasn't by my desk. I found her by the window instead; I know I left her by my desk. I was confused but didn't put too much thought about it as I rolled her back to my desk. I said, "Good morning," to her and waited for the students to come in. First bell rang- everyone was there by the time the final bell buzzed.

"Well, as you can all see we finally got our prize, her name is Lulu and she donated her body so we can learn from it, so let's treat her with respect and care."

I pushed her through the isles so everyone could see her up close. Most of the students touched her except one, Kat. She said that it felt like bad juju around Lulu (terrible wording) and she wouldn't touch her. I raised my eyebrows as I listened to her and then continued on through the isle. I rolled her back to beside my desk and picked up my book to start the day's lesson.

By the end of the day everyone had been introduced to her. I was so happy that the kids were pleased with her. I brought a shawl to wrap her up every night so she wouldn't get dusty. I placed her beside my desk and covered her up, then turned out the lights and locked up

Chapter 5

The several days went by. And every night Lulu was in a different place in the morning from where I'd left her the night before.

It was Tuesday morning, I turned on the lights in the classroom and Lulu was standing by the window with the shawl tied into a carrying sling. I know I'd left her by my desk just like before but once again she was moved.

Who was messing with her at night? I thought to myself. Then I went through the list of everyone who had a key to my room. There were several who had a key and could get into my room. Guess i'll start asking them to see who's messing with me. I'm sure it was one of them having a laugh. I moved Lulu as the class was piling in.

"Good morning class. Did anyone do anything exciting last night?"

Jacob raised his hand and said, "I cheesed puffed a lawn of my arch-enemy and since it rained last night his lawn is completely orange!" He said with a big smile.

I raised my eyebrows and smiled then said, "Creative, I give you an 8 on the scale of 10. How long does it last?" I asked.

"You planning on getting even with someone?" he asked.

The class all started razzing me, "Of course not! I would never do that!"

I said as I smiled and changed the subject. "So, does anyone know who's messing with Lulu every night? She keeps moving."

"Is that why she's got a sling on her?" One of the girls asked.

"Yes, someone thinks it's funny to dress her up I guess, anyway let's get down to business. We are going to go through the heart system today."

And with that class started. Classes came and went and finally it was lunch time, I was starving and ready to eat. Jet met me in the hallway and we walked together to the lunch room together.

"What's the special of the day?" I asked her.

"Roasted possum and mash potatoes." That meant it was mystery meat. We weren't sure what it was but it had a nice flavor to it. When we got to the cafeteria, I grabbed a tray and got into line then headed to the teachers lounge. The guys were really loud today—

"What's the question of the day guys?" they both stopped talking and looked at me.

"If you were stuck on a deserted island, what three things would you bring and why?"

I thought about it then said, "Flint stone for fire, a metal bucket for multi purposes and my best friend so he could keep me company, cause misery loves company." I said as a joke.

They asked Jet the same question.

"A hottie, a knife incase I need to kill him after awhile, and potato chips that never run out, got to have your salt intake." She said as she sat down to our table.

Then they went back to debating, "So, someone's messing with Lulu again. They must be really bored to keep moving her every day," I said as we settled.

"Why would anyone do that?" she said as she started eating.

"I don't know, probably a guy. You know how they are."

Jet looked at me seriously then said, "Maybe she's haunted."

Then she started laughing, "Yeah, maybe."

We finished our lunches then I stopped at the principal's office to ask him if he'd been messing with Lulu.

"Hey Rainey, what did I do for the pleasure of your company today?" he said sarcastically.

"Have you been in my room lately?"

He looked at me and shook his head, "Nope, why?"

"Someone's messing with my skeleton every night."

He stopped what he was doing and said, "Nope wasn't me."

"Ok, thanks. Let me know if you find out who it is. I'm sure someone's just having some fun with me," I said as I left for my room.

Well, that's one person off my list I thought as I walked upstairs to my room. I grabbed my sweater as I came in the room; it was a little cooler than before lunch, in fact you could see your breath, very strange!

At the end of the day, I wrapped Lulu up, said goodbye to her before I headed out. I ran into the track team running in the hallways 'cause it was raining outside. They all yelled hello as they went by. Sometimes I run with them just to keep in shape, maybe I'll do that tomorrow.

It was four by the time I pulled into the driveway. Miss Truet was outside getting bags out of her car, she was my crazy neighbor. She had her bra on the outside of her shirt today! She was one confused lady sometimes. She was in her early 60's and was raising four grandkids alone; I'd be crazy too I thought if I was her. I felt sorry for her; the grandkids were a very creative bunch of kids who were criminals in the making. I headed over to her to help with the bags.

"How's it going Miss T?" I said to her as I grabbed some bags.

"I thought you could use some help." I followed her into the house with the bags. Two of the grandkids were playing video games, they looked up at me, and then went back to shooting zombies mindlessly. I placed the bags on the table and went back out to get the rest. I set the bags down on the table. When I came back in, two of the boys were already going through the bag of food, they grabbed the potato chips, looked at me, said hi, then went back to the family room and started playing video games again.

"How's the teaching going?" she asked me.

"Great, I finally got my skeleton for the room."

She had been one of the neighbors that helped me save cans. I think they save more cans than the class.

"That's great. Is it a nice one?"

"Sure is. Next year, your grandkids will be using it too. How's it going for you? Do you need anything?"

She smiled and said, "No, we're doing well. One of the kids got a job and has been helping me with the bills."

I looked at her and asked, "What's the job they're doing?"

"Oh, it has something to do with the pawn shop." I smiled and thought about what one of the other neighbors said earlier this month- He'd said that a few of his lawn items had been stolen. Now I knew where they went. Oh, well I thought, Miss Truet needs the money more than the other neighbors needed the lawn things. And with that I said goodbye.

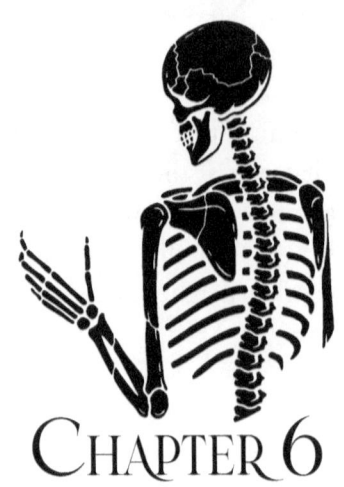

Chapter 6

The bell was ringing as I stepped into my classroom, my alarm clock didn't go off, and it was blinking when I got up, we must have had a power surge last night.

I apologized as I walked into the classroom; all of the students were talking. I noticed Lulu beside the window, it looked like she was looking out the window on the floor by her was the picture of her and the baby.

"Who's been messing with Lulu today?" I looked at the class,

"Please be careful with her." I said as I pulled her back to my desk and picked up the picture.

"So, I assume you all studied for the pop quiz today", all of the class stopped talking and looked at me.

"Another quiz? You enjoy torturing us don't you?" said one of the students as they put their books under their chair.

"It's an easy one if you read the chapter I assigned the other day. Please put your books on the floor."

I handed the test to Joel to pass out for me as I finished putting up my bag and coat in the closet.

"You have a half hour to finish. Go ahead and start."

I sat down in my chair and noticed Lulu was looking at me instead of the class. Strange, I thought she was facing the other direction. I sat down and graded some paper as the class worked on their test. Time flew by and before I knew it time was up for the quiz.

"Times up, I hope you all finished. Go ahead and bring them up to my desk, starting with this row."

I pointed to the row by the door. "You all may talk or play games for the rest of the hour. Please try to keep it under a loud roar; Mrs. Taylor said we interrupted her class the other day when we were talking."

When the bell rang it was time for lunch. I grabbed my bag and headed downstairs. I caught up with the gym teacher and we walked together the rest of the way to the lunch room. I brought my lunch today so I sat down in my normal seat and started eating. Jet and the band teacher walked into the room. Jet set down at my table. David, the gym teacher, sat at his table with the band leader. We all talked through lunch as we ate. The guys were debating as usual. Today's topic was which Aliens movie was the best.

After lunch, I was going to teach about the bones in the arm. So I pulled Lulu up to the board and put her arm up and drew arrows to the different bones. I dropped my chalk so I turned to get a new one and when I turned back Lulu was at the end of the black board instead of in the middle. I stood there looking at her.

"I must be getting tired," I said to myself out loud as I pulled her back to the middle of the board and finished. The rest of the day went by quickly, I closed all the windows, watered the plants then wrapped Lulu up in the shawl and went home.

Charlie pulled up a few minutes after I got home. We ended up going to dinner. We headed to our favorite Mexican place, El Arrio's, for chips and salsa. They have the best cheese dip in the whole town and their guacamole is made right at your table. We sat down and they served the chips, we ordered drinks then started talking.

"So, tell me all about your field trip to the library, did you find what you were looking for?" he started talking with a mouthful of chips.

"Yeah, I think I almost have enough on women's health now, I say that every time then I find more things to add. I might end up just doing a smaller book and have it just about women's stuff." He said as he took a drink.

"I'm looking forward to reading it, I'm sure it will be interesting."

He told me all about what he had found out the library and then asked me, "What's new with you?"

I finished my drink and then said, "Don't laugh but I'm beginning to think my skeleton is haunted."

He started laughing.

"I said, don't laugh." I hit him with my hand in the shoulder.

"Well, maybe it's just one of my friends having a laugh making Lulu move all over my room at night."

I took a bite of chips.

"It could happen I guess, stranger things have happened to others. If it is haunted, maybe I'll write a book about it." he said with a smirk.

"Well, it would make for interesting reading I guess." I said. We finished up our food then he walked me to my car, gave me a hug and kissed my cheek and said goodbye, "I'll call you tomorrow. Have a good night." And he walked to his car. I thought about Lulu all the way home.

Zeba and the ferret were waiting by the door for me when I walked into the house. Guess they were hungry.

"Sorry guys, did I forget to fill your bowl again?" I asked as I grabbed the cat food out of the cabinet.

They ran to the bowl and started eating. I put up my leftovers in the fridge then headed upstairs to get into my pjs. I worked around the house cleaning and doing a load of laundry for awhile. By the time it looked good it was late so I went upstairs and got into bed.

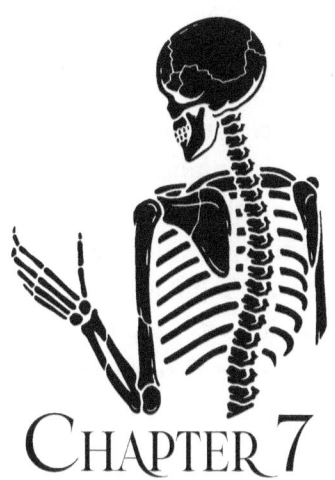

Chapter 7

The day flew by at school; it was lunch time before I knew it. I ate but I'm not sure what it was, it had a good after taste though. I walked with Jet to my room and she came in to get a book that I had brought her that was on the art of zenology.

When we open the door and went in the black board was covered with the word, "मेरा बच्चा".

It was written all over the board. We looked at each other then I said, "What in the world? Someone really has a lot of time on their hands to do this."

I had told her about how someone was moving Lulu around the room the other day.

"Well, I guess they're getting creative anyways." She went to look at Lulu up close, and then said, "She really is a nice one. You got lucky she's got all her teeth too; most of the time they don't. Hey look at her closely down in the pelvic area she's got a crack in her pelvic bone."

I walked over to look, "Well, I wonder what happened to her?"

After a long pause Jet said, "Well, have fun cleaning the board I got to go and thanks again for the book." Then as she was heading for the door.

"I hope you find out who's doing this."

"Yeah, me too."

The bell rang and class started piling in. I waited for everyone to get there then pointed to the board and asked the class, "So, who's the one that's been moving Lulu around and writing on my board?"

I looked around, eyeing the class, trying to get someone to talk.

"I'm not mad I think it's kind of funny that one of you has gone through so much time and effort."

No one said anything so I said, "Well, I guess no ones going to talk unless I bribe you huh? So I'll let whoever is doing this get out of a test, if they own up to it now." And with that I turned around and headed to the board to erase it. No one owned up sadly.

The day went on and I gave the same speech to each class. No one took the blame, but I was sure someone would the next time I gave a test. The day was almost over so I packed up my books as the bell was ringing.

I said goodbye to all the kids as they left and rolled Lulu back to the place by my desk. After everyone was gone, I went to the closet to grab my sweater and bag and when I turned around I ran into Lulu- I almost knocked her down.

"What in the world? How did you get over here?"

I was completely at a loss.

"I know you were just by my desk-how did you…? Someone's got to be messing with me but how did they do that?"

I shook my head as I rolled her back to my desk. "Now, stay here, no more moving."

I was a little shook up as I turned off the lights. I ran into the janitor as I was locking up.

"Very funny", I said to him.

"What?" he asked.

"Did you just do that? It wasn't funny." I said as I put my hands on my hips.

"I don't know what you're talking about Rainey," he stated.

"You didn't just move my skeleton?"

I raised my eyebrows then he said, "Of course not, why would I do that?"

I stared at him then said, "I'm sorry but someone's messing with me and I thought it was you. Do you clean in here every night?" I asked.

"Not every night no, but usually I'm in here twice a week." He said as he grabbed his broom.

"Ok, please be careful with my skeleton, Lulu, she's brand new and it took a lot of cans to get her." I said as I started walking.

"Will do. Have a good night" He said as he waved good night to me.

I was totally freaked out as I walked down the hall. How in the world did Lulu move behind me I wondered?

I was in deep thought as I drove home and still shook up. Something was happening in my room and I wasn't sure I liked it. I needed peeps and coffee to calm me down. I stopped at the store on the way home. The store had Halloween candy on sale so I decided to grab a few bags for trick or treaters and my classroom. I choose Peeps, lots of them, a bag of Laffy Taffy, Sixlets, Mary Jane's and a mixed bag of chocolates. I also got pumpkin spice coffee I paid then got in my car and tore open the peeps; I shoved them into my mouth.

Heaven, true heaven I thought to myself as I chewed the marshmallows. By the time I got home I had a lot of empty wrappers in the car. I grabbed them and went in. I had the Peeps half gone by the time I was inside.

I sat down at the table and finished them and my coffee. After that I grabbed a glass of wine and took a big drink from it. I played over all the details of all the things that have been happening since I got Lulu. I was still having issues knowing that it was a possibility that my skeleton could be haunted. I was almost sure of it now. It had to be, what else could be going on? I was in deep thought when the phone rang. I grabbed it and said "hello", it was Charlie.

I told Charlie what happened and we went over it again and again then he said, "Well, gang I think we have another mystery on our hands Scooby Doo!" he said in his best Scooby Doo voice.

I laughed, "I guess we do. Better get some Scooby snacks."

We talked for a few more minutes. I was calm when I got off the phone. I took out my notebook and went to work writing down all the things that have happened with Lulu. I had little notes about each incident and wrote who had been there to see it too. I thought a lot about it all as the night went on. It was getting late so not knowing for sure what to do, I headed to bed to read, it always calms my head.

Zeba jumped into bed with me and soon the ferret joined us too. I picked up my book, looked at the title – ghost stories from haunted historical places, I laid it down and grabbed another book. I couldn't read the scary one tonight with all that's going on in my room.

Finally at midnight I put the alarm on. The ferret was snuggled up in zebas paws. I pet them both good night and turned off the light. We all fell asleep together on the bed. I dreamed about Lulu and the baby on and off all night.

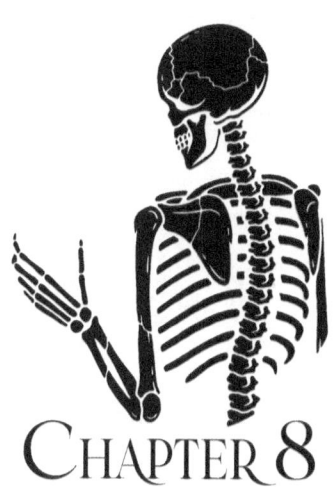

Chapter 8

The next morning, I woke to the ferret licking my cheek, I think he thinks I'm a salt lick. I got dressed then picked up the ferret, kissed him on the ear then carried him downstairs with me. I could smell the coffee halfway down the stairs.

I filled up the food bowl for the fuzzy little guys then made myself a jelly egg sandwich, my favorite. I finished up then grabbed my coffee and headed back to school to face another day in paradise. It was a sunny fall day; I grabbed my sunglasses and got in the car. I made it to school in record time, must be my lucky day because I got all green lights on the way there.

I ran into Miss Fergusson on the way into the school. We caught up talking as we walked. It's too bad that we don't have lunch together, I really enjoy her company. She asked how Charlie was and I told her that we really need to get together soon. I stopped at the office to get my mail and pick up some of the papers that I had the secretary copy for me. I grabbed them all and walked to my room. When I got there I hung up my things and got ready for the day.

We were going to be studying the bones in the hand today so I moved Lulu up to the board and extended her hand so I could draw arrows to the bones. I placed her right hand up and started labeling as the final bell rang. Everyone was in their seats.

"You all ready for today? We are going to be studying the bones in the arm. Can you hand these out please?" I said as I handed one on the students the papers.

I turned around to head back to the board to finish labeling the arm, and Lulu's arm was down and the left arm was up!

"What the heck? Did anyone see that?" the students just looked at me.

"What happened? What are you talking about?" asked one of the kids in the front row.

"Her arm just…"

I shook my head in disbelief and said, "Oh, never mind."

Put her right arm back up and put her left down and started labeling again. I finished and sat down at my desk and waited for all the kids to finish their papers.

Micah raised her hand and asked, "What part of the arm is baby suppose to be?"

I looked at her the board, it said baby beside the rest of the labeling. I got up to erase it.

I said, "Sorry, I guess I have other things on my mind."

The bell rang and I stepped out into the hallway with the kids, everyone but one girl was out of the room heading to their next period of classes. I was talking with the teacher from the room next to mine and that's when I heard it, a loud scream coming from my room. I ran back to my door and looked in.

One of the girls, Kat, was yelling and was visibly shaking. I went to her to comfort her and find out what was wrong.

"Lulu-her head just moved, I saw her move! She was moving on her own!"

I looked at her and touched her shoulder trying to calm her down, "It's ok. Are you sure she moved? It's going to be ok. She's just a skeleton, she can't move by herself." I said to her.

"No, she moved I saw her."

"Ok, it's alright now- calm down. Everything's going to be ok." I told her but I was just as freaked out as she was but I was trying to remain calm for her sake.

"Lets get out of here and I'll walk you to your next class."

We talked as we walked to her next class. She was better by the time the bell rang. I headed back to my classroom; the kid's were all asking what had happened.

I told them and that's when Joel said, "I told you she has bad juju. Maybe we should send her back and get another one, one without juju issues."

He said with a serious face, "We're not sending her back I'm sure someone's just messing with her that's all. It's no big deal."

"Maybe she's haunting us because she didn't want to be hung up in a health room for the rest of eternity," Said one of the other girls.

A couple of the other kids chimed in and agreed with her. "Ok, I'm sure it's not haunted and if it is maybe we just need to find out what the unsettled business is and fix them. Ok, let's get back to class."

We went through chapter seven in the health book and then I asked one of the kids if they would water the plants in our room for me. After a few minutes class was up.

The next class was on a caffeine buzz and it took a lot out of me. They kept talking as we watched a movie about the heart. I moved Lulu to the back of the room so we could put the screen up in the front of the room.

We were half way through the movie when Tommy yelled out, "Quit touching me"

I looked up and told him to be quiet and we went back to watching the movie. He yelled again and I asked him what was going on.

He said, "Someone keeps touching my hair and it's bugging me."

"There's no one behind you Tommy, just Lulu and I'm sure she's not doing it."

It's almost time to leave, we'll finish up the movie tomorrow. I flipped the light on and turned off the movie.

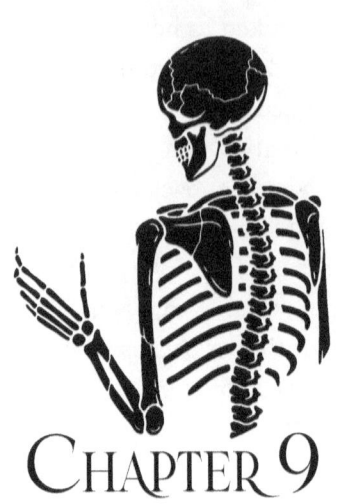

Chapter 9

It was Friday and so far it had been a great day. Lunch was good and I had lots of happy campers due to me bringing in cookies for the classroom for their reward for doing well on their test. We were all eating cookies when the fire alarm went off.

"Ok, class you know the drill, everyone line up and we'll walk to the parking lot together. Just take your bags with you and leave everything else." I said to them as we headed out the door. As always it was chaos in the hallway to get down stairs.

It was beautiful outside so no one complained about standing outside for the next hour. We all talked and wondered what happened. The fire trucks came so I guess something had happened but no one knew what it was yet.

Finally the fire marshal told us it was safe for us to head back inside. When I walked in the doorway of my room I couldn't believe my eyes, everything was a mess. Papers were thrown all over the place, chairs upside down my desk drawers were opened and half dumped out. The plants hanging from the ceiling were on the floor with dirt spilled all over the place. It was a train wreck.

"What the heck happened?" I said out loud to all who were listening.

The kids just looked and they were in total disbelief too.

"Maybe the wind blew them over."

One of the kids said as she pointed to the windows that were opened.

"I don't think the wind could do all this." I said as I pointed around the room.

"Wow!" Micah said as he walked in and noticed what everyone was staring at.

"What the freak?" he yelled as he headed to his desk.

"Well, I guess turn your chairs back up right and who wants to work on cleaning up the plants? Someone else can help pick up papers." I said to the class.

Everyone was talking as they worked on cleaning up the mess.

"I just don't know who would do this to us."

It took awhile to clean up the room but finally we got it done.

At the end of the day, I went to Jets room and vented to her. She said the same thing I said, "Why would anyone do that?" she asked me if I ticked off anyone lately or flunked a student.

I said no to both of them. "Not to change the subject but what do you think of the lantern? Do you like the colors?" I looked at them then picked it up and admired the craftsmanship of it. It was beautiful.

"It's all yours after tomorrow. You can hang in your room or take it home."

I thanked her for making it for me.

"Well, I'm gonna take off, I'll see you tomorrow. Hopefully no one messes with my room again."

I smiled and left to go home. I thought about what happened at school all through the drive. I called Charlie on the way home and asked him to come over for dinner. He accepted.

"I'll see you soon." And I hung up.

When I got home Miss Truet was trying to get her youngest grandkid out of the tree, the littlest one of the four liked to climb trees when she was upset. This time she had climbed really high and was throwing pickles at her grandma. I waved to her and asked if she needed help. She said no that Lillie was almost out of pickles and she'd climb down eventually. So I waved goodbye and headed inside.

When Charlie got there we hung out on the deck out back. "Wow, it's really coming along back here." He pointed to the rock wall.

"So, what's going on with you? What else happen at school today?"

I nodded my head in disbelief then went on to tell him what happened over the last few weeks.

"Well, I'm starting to believe Lulu is haunting you, but the question is why she is haunting you?"

We both just stared at each other.

"I don't know, but apparently she has some unfinished business with her life. What should I do to figured it out?" I wondered out loud.

"First, we need to find out where she came from and how she died. Then we can start filling in the gaps from her life."

Charlie was the perfect person to help solve this mystery and research Lulu's life. We made a plan over the next hour and Charlie made a list of what I needed to find out and do. We ordered a pizza as we talked. It was a perfect day to eat outside alfresco. We ordered from Bazbo's Pizza, they had gourmet pizzas so much better than normal pepperoni pizza.

I ordered cherry peppers, tomatoes and spinach with goat cheese pizza drizzled with vinegar and oil, it had a kick to it. By the time the pizza guy arrived, we had a plan all worked out to figure what we should do. We pigged out on pizza and had a few drinks. By the time we finished, it was ten o'clock so Charlie took off and I went inside to put away the leftovers in the fridge. As I was walking through the kitchen I noticed the picture of Lulu and the baby on the counter top by the phone.

I picked it up and looked at it, "That's it—," I said out loud to myself, finally a clue. In the corner of the picture, there was the name of what must be the hospital.

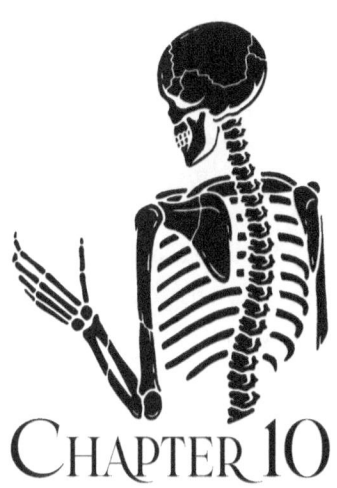

Chapter 10

It was Saturday so I slept in then ate a late breakfast. I had all my running around that I put off during the week to do so I got dressed and headed out. It was a bright sunny day outside and The Lawn Nazi was at it again, he waved as I walked to my car.

I wish he'd mow my lawn, it wasn't my favorite thing to do. I mow once, maybe once or twice a month, but at least my yard had trees in it; his didn't have one tree, he said he didn't like the mess trees made. He did have a point there but my backyard is prettier though.

It was like an English garden and I loved my rock wall. I drove to the library to look up The Red Market and see what I could find out about it.

By four o'clock I found just about everything that the library had to offer about it. I found some addresses and phone numbers of different companies that collected bodies and how they marketed them. I knew when I went that they made contracts with people and paid the families of the deceased when they collected the bodies.

I made copies of everything I thought that would help me find out the history of Lulu and her family. I asked the resource lady at the desk if there was anything else about The Red Market at the other branch of the library and she looked it up for me.

"They have three books on it. Do you want me to have them send them over here or do you want to pick them up at that branch?" she inquired.

"How late are they opened today?" I asked her.

"Till five, you'll have to hurry if you want it today; they close in a half hour." She smiled at me.

"Well, when can you have it here for me to pick up here because I'm not going to make it there by five with traffic?"

"Yes, I'm afraid you won't. We can have it here by Monday or Tuesday. Is that alright for you?"

I nodded to her yes.

"That will be fine. Thank you."

I gave my library card to her and she ordered them for delivery to here.

"Thanks again," I said as I left.

I carried my bag and my papers to the car go into the car and called Charlie to tell him what I found. He told me some of the things he found out about the market on the internet while he was researching. Between the both of us I think we'll figure out what we need to know.

When I got home I made a call to the phone numbers I found on the paper at the library to see what I could find out but with it being the weekend I didn't get far. They told me to call back during the weekday. So, with that I resigned to trying to research further and called my mom. I hadn't talked to her much since all the things started happening at school. I'd been consumed with it all. We talked for a while; I told her what's been going on.

She was very interested; she loved ghost stories and told me I should call the local ghost hunters to see what they could do. She said it would make a great half hour show." I laughed at her and said "yeah, that's what I need my friends to think I've lost my marbles. It's bad enough that the kids at school are talking about it all." She told me to stop by for dinner anytime and she loved me. With that I said goodbye.

The rest of the weekend dragged on and on. I was consumed with thoughts of Lulu and what her history held. I was going over all the information I found out about The Red Market at the library. I was organizing all the papers and notes on the table when Zeba jumped up on the table. She sat down on the papers and started pawing the picture of Lulu and the baby. She pulled it up into her paws and started purring.

"Whatcha doing there Zeba? You loving them? Are they your kittens? Huh baby?"

I sat there petting her then I had an aha moment.

"That's it Zeba! You're a genius." I rubbed her head, then said

"Lulu had a baby-that's her baby in the picture. Maybe something happened to the both of them. You're so smart Zeba, thank you."

I picked her up and hugged her. I picked up the picture and looked at it again. This time I noticed how she was holding the baby, in a sling with her scarf. Just like she how I found her in my class room. I also looked over the name in the corner of the picture. Finally it was all coming together. Come Monday hopefully I can get more information from the company that sold her to me.

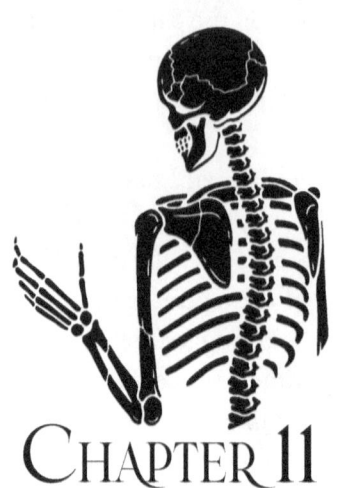

Chapter 11

Monday finally arrived, I woke earlier than my alarm because I was excited about finally getting to make some calls. I showered then headed downstairs. The smell of coffee was lingered in the air; it was hazelnut so the whole kitchen smelled wonderful. I poured myself a cup of coffee and grabbed a croissant and some honey, then sat down at the table.

My ferret, Little Cobb was already at my feet begging for food. I gave him a little piece then rubbed his ear and went back to drinking my coffee. I grabbed my folder full of information and put it in my bag to take to school. I'd hopefully get through to the company who sold Lulu to me during my lunch break.

When I got to school, I stopped at the office to pick up my mail. I ran into the janitor, he told me he wasn't going to clean my room anymore because of what happened to him last Friday.

I looked at him and asked, "What happened? What are you talking about?"

I looked at him confused.

"I was in your room cleaning the floors listening to my headphones like I always do when the lights suddenly went off and someone or something grabbed the back of my neck. That's when my headset went flying through the air and I heard this voice, sounded like a woman's voice but it was in a different dialect say, 'My baby!' I was so scared

I couldn't move for a second then I turned and ran for the hallway. I was scared outta my wits!"

I stood there looking at him not knowing what to say.

Then he added, "I'm not going back in your room ever!"

"I can't believe it! That's so weird. I don't know what to say. Are you alright? Did it hurt you?" I asked him.

"No, I'm ok but I'm really freaked out by it. I don't even want to be here alone at night to clean anymore." I nodded my head and agreed.

I couldn't blame him. So far nothing's happened to me; it just freaks me out but it takes a lot to really scare me.

"I'm so sorry." I said as I touch his arm.

"I just don't know what else to say."

Then he added, "I and the other janitor are gonna clean together for awhile but neither of us wants to go in to your room. I'm sorry the day janitor will be taking over your room."

"Yes, I agree, that's fine."

The first bell rang.

"I have to get to class. I'm so sorry that that had to happen to you." And I left in a hurry. Omg! My room is haunted; I believe that now without a doubt. I walked slowly to my room and replayed the whole conversation over in my head as I walked. This is getting serious; I have to find out what happened with Lulu or no ones going to want to be in my room.

I walked into the room when the second bell went off and stood there looking at Lulu. "What happened to you Lulu? I'm trying to help you." I said to her quietly.

Joel was standing behind me and asked me, "Is it true what everyone's saying about your room? Is it haunted?"

I looked at him and said, "I don't know but there's some weird things going on in here."

"Yeah I heard about the janitor the other night. I told you Lulu has bad juju."

"I'm sure everything will work out." I told him as I shooed him to his seat. Everyone was talking still after the bell.

"Class, calm down. Its time to get settled for now. I hope you all had a great weekend."

One of the girls in the front row raised her hand and asked me, "So, is all this stuff they're saying really happening in our room?"

I looked around as everyone got quiet waiting for me to say something. I cleared my throat then said, "I'm sure it's been all blown up from the truth." I assured them.

"Is any of it true then?" she asked again.

"I admit that something's have happened that I can't explain but I'm sure were fine and have nothing to worry about. I am trying to find out the truth. I'll let you know when I know."

They all just sat there looking at me and then I said, "time for class." I thought to myself I've got to figure it out or no ones going to want to be in my room anymore.

Lunch time couldn't come soon enough. Finally I could go make some calls. I rushed down to the office to use the phone. I took out the notes I made and placed the first call to the company that I bought Lulu from. After being on hold for fifteen minutes I got to talk to a person, finally. I didn't get far with her so I asked to speak to the manager in charge.

After waiting another 10 minutes they got on the phone, "Hello, May I help you?" the manager asked.

"Yes, I recently bought a full skeleton from your company and I was wondering if you could give me so information of its history and where it came from. I bought it for my health class, I'm a teacher."

She cleared her throat then said. "Well, I can help you some of it but you'll need to talk with the other company that buys them and the company that collects and gets donors."

"What can you tell me?" I asked her.

"I'll need to know the name of the skeleton first off, that's how we register them and the number on the card."

Then I said, "Ok, her name is Lulu and she came with a picture of her and a baby. Her number is 4242"

She took the name and the number that was on the card and ran it through the computer as I waited.

After a few minutes she told me, "Alright, I have where it came from and what company we bought her from. She came from Exoskeletons out of Canada."

She waited for me to say something.

"Great, do you have a number for it?"

"Yes, of course I can give you that."

After taking down the number, I asked if there was anything else she could tell me. She said that's all that she had. I'd have to call the other company. I thanked her and hung up. I looked at my watch I didn't have time to make the other call so I hustled to the lounge and ate as fast as I could. I only had fifteen minutes left of lunch time. I'd have to make the other call tomorrow or try tonight at home if they're still opened. I finished lunch as I told Jet what I found out. She wished me luck for the next call and we headed to our classes. The rest of the day flew by and it was time to head back home. I wrapped Lulu up and told her goodnight like I did every night.

By the time I got home after running some errands it was five o'clock. I figured the company would be closed by tried it anyways. It rang several times then went straight to voice mail. I hung up, I'll try again tomorrow.

I called Charlie and told him what I found out. He said that was great and I should find out more tomorrow and to be patient. He said he found out the name of two companies that sell skeletons to the place that I bought her from. So tomorrow I'd be making two calls. I thanked him and told him goodnight and that I'd call him when I found something out.

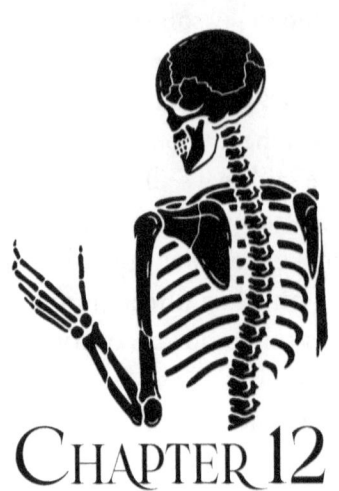

Chapter 12

By morning, I had a one tracked mind, I couldn't wait to make the calls. I was in such a state that I almost forgot to feed the little fuzzy ones.

I dumped a cup of cat food in the bowl and put a carrot in there for Little Cobb, I filled up their water bowl and my thermos with coffee and left for school. I was hoping maybe I would have time to make a call before class started. I got to the office and went in the little room that's for teachers to work. I was lucky no one was in there. I called the company Exoskeletons first. I was on hold for five minutes then a woman answered the phone.

"Thanks for holding what can I do for you?" she asked in an accent.

"Hello, my names Rainey and I'd like to get some information on a skeleton that I purchased."

"What exactly do you want to know?"

"Well, I bought this skeleton from the company that your company sells to and I'd like to find out where she came from, and where she had donated herself to in the first place. Could you help me with that?" I waited for a reply.

"Sure I need the name of the skeleton, the number on the tag and the company you bought her from." She said cheerfully.

I gave her all the information and she placed me on hold. First bell rang while I waited. Finally she came back on line then said, "I found out what company she was donated to and the place she went through to sell her body. They are both in India."

"That's great!" I said.

"Do you have the numbers and the addresses for those places?" She gave me them all and asked if she could help with anything else. I said no and thanked her. The final bell rang as I hung up. Yeah, I was finally getting somewhere with all of this. I grabbed my things and raced upstairs. I apologized to the class for being late and with that we started class.

As soon as the bell rang for lunch I headed back to the office to make another call. My cell phone buzzed as I was walking; there was a message from the library, my books were ready to be picked up today. I'd swing by after school to pick them up. When I got to the office the phone was being used and they said it was going to be awhile. So I decided to head to the lunch room instead. When I opened the door the guys were really loud.

"What's up you too? What's the question of the day?" I said to them.

They both said in unison, "Ghost. And if they're real." Coach looked at me and asked, "With all that's happening in your room, do you believe now?"

I nodded my head and added, "Yes, I think that it is very likely that ghost do exist."

And with that I sat down. I was kind of quiet while we ate thinking about all the stuff that's going on and trying to put it all together. Jet babbled most of the lunchtime and I simply nodded and agreed with most of what she was saying.

When the final bell buzzed, I grabbed my things and headed straight to the library to pick up my books that were being held. As soon as I got home I started going through them. There were three of them, so I leafed through them all.

There was a chapter about where most of the skeletons come from and how much each person's family or themselves get paid before or after. I guess you can get paid before you donate your body or your family can get paid later after they collect the body, the latter pays better. Plus they had a chapter that was all about selling your organs too. There was a website address in two of the books so I went to them and read through the site.

It was very helpful to understand the process of what happens to each body. Plus it mentions the few companies that are legal and those that aren't. I guess there's a huge black market on all of the Red Market things. It took most of the evening to go through all the stuff but it was worth it. I had a lot better understanding of it now. I closed up around ten and headed to bed.

Zeba was already on the pillow asleep. A few minutes after I got into bed Little Cobb joined us on the bed, we all fell asleep together. I dreamed about Lulu and her Baby. I woke in the middle of the night crying; my dream had seemed almost real and it was very vivid. Lulu in my dream asked me to find her baby for her; she said they had been separated by the company after they donated.

I sat up in bed thinking about what had happened in my dream. Was this a vision or just a dream I wondered. I had a hard time falling back to sleep after that. After a few hours of tossing and turning I gave up on sleep and got up. It was five in the morning.

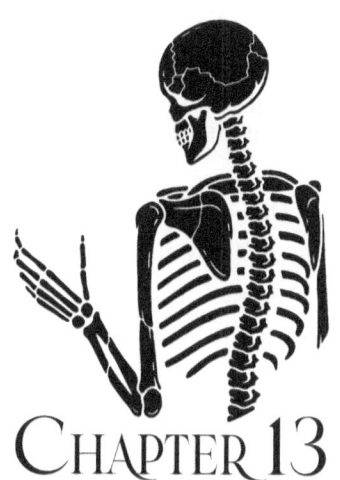

Chapter 13

I called the next company on the list since it was in India, I didn't know what time it was there so I made the call early in the morning our time. It was the middle of the day there so they were opened for business.

"Hallo-can I help you this is Kadjidia who do I speak with?" she said in a thick accent that was hard to understand.

"Yes, I'm trying to find out about the skeleton that came from your company. I need to know where she came from and who donated her."

"Oh, yes we might to help you; I need the companies' name that you bought her from and the name on the card and number on the back. When was it bought?" she inquired.

"I bought her almost a month ago and here is the number and names." She went over the information with me several times because I couldn't understand her very well.

After a few minutes she said, "Here's is the number of store we had her from."

She told me as I wrote it all down.

Then I said, "Was she the only donor? Was she alone when she came in?"

"Call the number for more help. I can help no more. Thank you come again."

And she hung up on me. Well, at least I got some more leads. It was taking a lot more time then I thought it was going to but I'm slowly getting to the bottom of it all.

I called the other company since I still had time. It rang forever before anyone answered it.

"Hallo," he said, "this is Badri I can help you what is that you need?" he seemed happy enough but hard to understand too.

"Yes, I have a number and the name of a skeleton from which I bought from your company. The other company Exoskeleton said that your company is the donor collection center."

"Mmm... yes, what is that you need?" he asked me.

"I'm trying to find out who donated the skeleton that I bought and if she was the only body donated at the time."

He told me, "Yes, it will take some time and research to get all of that. We call you back with it. Your number please?"

I gave him the number then he said it would take a day or so to get back with me. I thanked him and said good bye.

I got to school early the next day, so I could watered the plants and straightened up in there since no one was cleaning it every day. I had to do some light cleaning in there. I took out the Lysol and sprayed each of the desks.

When I got to the one in the back of the room, it was covered with the word baby and just as I read it out loud Lulu's skeleton rattled. I looked up and her head that had been facing the window was completely turned around backwards and it was facing me. I looked down at the desk and it moved two inches from me. I jumped back.

I stood there not knowing what to do then I said, "I hear you, Lulu, I'm trying to help you. Give me sometime."

I walked up to the front of the room and fixed Lulus head and placed her by my desk. The kids would be coming soon so I went to the bathroom to compose myself. By the time I got back to my room most of the kids were in their seats chatting loudly.

We went through the entire chapter on the digestive system and finished up just as the bell rang for lunch. I walked down to the lunch room with the kids. We joked about the mystery meat that we'd all be eating for our lunches. When we got there they all let me cut in front of them in the line, then I headed to the teachers lounge to eat. I was hoping I'd get a call from the company but so far nothing.

The guys were going over the top b rated movies that some of the bigger stars made before they made it big. I mentioned Killer Clowns from Outer Space; it freaked me out when I was a kid. The coach had seen it before and agreed that it was a little scary when he was younger. Jet said she'd never heard of it but it sounded fun.

We all started teasing each other over what we were eating for the rest of the lunch hour. We all came up with what we thought it might be. Possum, rat, road kill and cat were among our choices.

"Yummy, yummy" I said.

The bell rang soon after that. Jet and I walked to the office together to pick up our mail. Neither of us got anything exciting so we headed to the classroom. Right before we walked out the secretary told me that a company that was the donor center called and left a number and name of a girl to call her back. She handed me the memo and I took it with me.

The remained of the day dragged on and on, I couldn't wait to go home. I was hoping that they the company would still be open when I got home. I grabbed my things, wrapped Lulu up and told her I'd have some news by tomorrow hopefully. And with that I turned off the lights and went home.

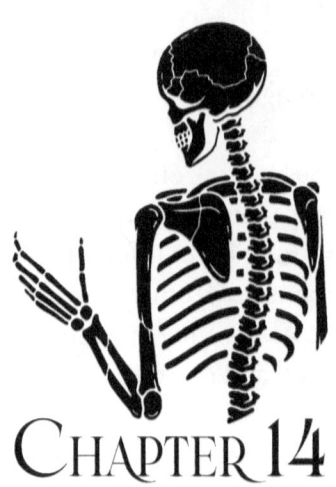

Chapter 14

It was getting chilly outside and the wind had picked up by the time I was home. I went in and poured myself a glass of wine to relax with. I took out my menus from the restaurants that had take out, to see which one I wanted. I narrowed it down to Chinese and Thai.

They both sounded good so I tossed them in the air to see which one landed on the table and I'd order from that one. Chinese, it was. I picked out a few items then called it in and they said it would be twenty minutes. I took off my shoes and went upstairs to change into my yoga pants and a sweatshirt, then headed back downstairs to finish up my glass of wine. I went through the pile of mail that I'd left there since yesterday. I got several magazines so I was happy. I took them and the bottle of wine to my recliner and relaxed waiting for my dinner to arrive.

I had just finished looking through one of the magazines and started the second one when the doorbell rang. I paid the man for delivering my food and camped out in the family room eating on my chair; I watched a horror movie while I ate. I pigged out then sat in a food coma watching the rest of the movie.

After the movie, I headed upstairs to get ready for bed. I lay down and got all cozy in the blankets to read for awhile. Zeba joined me on the bed after a few minutes. My phone rang as I was reading, it was Charlie, he called to ask me what I'd found out about Lulu. I told him everything I found out and that I was waiting to call back from the donor company in the morning. He said that was great that I had found out what I did already. I told him about the books from the library and the information that I got out of the company. He'd found out some things as well on his own.

After a few minutes, I told him I'd call him as soon as I found out who donated her and if she was alone. He said he'd be waiting to hear back from me and with that we hung up. I went back to reading and before long it was midnight and I was falling asleep holding my book. I turned out the lights and fell into a deep sleep. I dream the same dream about Lulu and the baby again.

This time Lulu was giving birth to the baby and the last thing I remember was the Dr. saying, "I'm sorry."

Then I woke up. She must be trying to tell me what happened.

My alarm was due to go off just as Zeba and Little Cobb ran across my chest on the bed, they were playing chase.

"Thanks guys for waking me up!" I yelled at them as they jumped off the bed and ran in a circle around the bed.

I got up and went to wash my face to wake up and put on my make-up. It was supposed to be chilly today so I put on my thick sweater and a long plaid skirt and boots. I grabbed Little Cobb as I headed to the stairs and carried him down with me.

When I got to the kitchen I stopped at the fridge and got him a little piece of cheese, then filled the cat bowl with food. I headed to the coffee maker to pour myself a cup full. After a few minutes, when I woke up I went ahead and made the call to the lady from the donor center. I was hoping that all my questions would finally be answered.

The phone rang several times then a woman answered on the other end of the line. "Yes, I'm trying to get a hold of Khiesa- she called me and told me to call her back."

"This is Khisea can I help you?"

"I sure hope you can. I'm trying to find out about a skeleton that I ordered from your company. I gave all the information to the other women that I spoke with the other day."

There was a pause then she said, "Yes, she had given me the information and I have some answers for you."

I had a big smile on my face, now I'm going to get somewhere I thought. "That's great! What can you tell me?"

"Yes, her family had given her up at the request of her before she died, so she could help with the money problem that her family was going through. She came in with three other bodies the day she arrived."

"Really, is it possible for me to get the families name and address and number? I'd like to help her family since she is an asset to my class room I'd like to repay her."

"It's highly unusual but I can call the family to see if they would allow it." she said.

"That would be great. Thank you. Will you call me or should I wait for you to contact me back?"

"No, I will contact you. It will take a few days to get it all situated. I shall call your number you gave me."

I thanked her and hung up.

By the time I got off the phone I only had fifteen minutes till school started, I was running late. I grabbed everything and hurried out the door, I was late by the time I got there. My class was sitting there talking loudly when I walked in.

"I'm sorry, I had an urgent call from India. Everyone settle down and take out your book, we're going to review the last chapter then have a short quiz on it before the end of the hour."

After the quiz, one of the girls from the school newspaper talked to me she was interested in doing a story on our class and how we worked together to get Lulu. Plus she added with all the things going on in our room since we got Lulu might be a wonderful Halloween issue.

I told her I'd be delighted to talk to her about that but I was a little hesitant to talk about the haunting. She assured me that all of the kids who knew about it were fascinated and curious about it, so it would be good to set the record straight. She said she'd get back to me and that she would like to take a picture to go along with the story as well.

The rest of the day my mind was busy thinking about waiting to hear back from the lady from the donor center. I was really hoping that Lulu's family would talk to me or at least take a call from me.

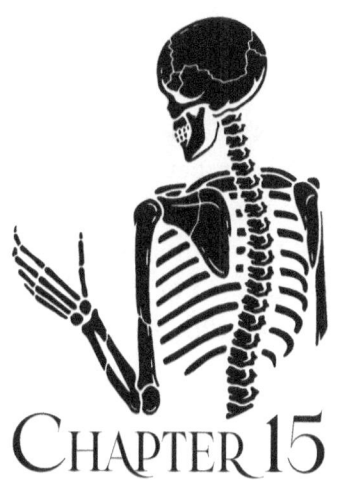

Chapter 15

Several days went by without any word than finally on Wednesday there was a call for me during lunch time. It was Khiesa calling me back. Luckily for me I was close to the office when she called.

The secretary called out the door and told me, so I ran back to the office to answer.

"Yes, this is Rainey. Thank you for calling me back. What were you able to find out for me?" I waited for her to speak.

"Yes, I found out that Lulu was donated along with two other bodies. I talked with the family of hers and they said they would be happy to talk with you. They wondered where they went and they would like to find out from you. Here is the number for you to call and the address for you as well."

I wrote down all the information from her then thanked her several times before I hung up.

"I'm so excited!" I said to the secretary as I walked out of the office.

By the end of the day I couldn't wait to call Charlie and share all that I found out, he'd be thrilled for me. I told Lulu I was going to be talking with her family and that I was planning on helping them with some of their money issues as I covered her up and placed her by the window since she almost always ended up there in the morning. I told her good night then left for the evening.

I called Charlie as soon as I got to my car, he picked up on the third ring.

"Charlie, guess what?" I said excitedly.

"What's up? Did you get some news?"

"Yes, finally I found out that Lulu was donated with three other bodies and I got the number for her family so I can call them direct."

"Really? Oh that's wonderful! So when will you call them?"

"I'm a little nervous, I'm not sure what to say to them but I'm looking forward to speaking with them all the same." I said to him.

"Do you want to meet for dinner tonight? I'm too revved up to go home right now." I said.

"Sure, meet at the usual place?" he asked me.

"Of course, where else would we go?"

"Ok, meet you there in twenty minutes." he said then hung up. I made it cross town in no time and pulled up right as he was walking to the door.

"Hey you! Where ya going?"

He turned and smiled at me. I gave him a big hug and we walked in together. They greeted us then they seat us in a booth, we were in there so much they knew what we would order all the time.

The server brought us our beers and some cheese dip with salsa. We ordered two grilled chicken quesadillas with guacamole. We started on the chips after we ordered. I told him all about the phone call. We went over it several times because I was so excited.

He also helped me figure out what to say when I talk to Lulu's family. I told him I would be calling them in the morning. Dinner came and we talked and ate then after dinner we said goodbye and he walked me to my car. He wished me luck with the call tomorrow and then I headed home. It was late when I got there, Zeba was waiting by the door, guess she was hungry or her bowl was empty. I went to fill it up and put the leftovers on the table and went upstairs to bed; I was beat from a long day.

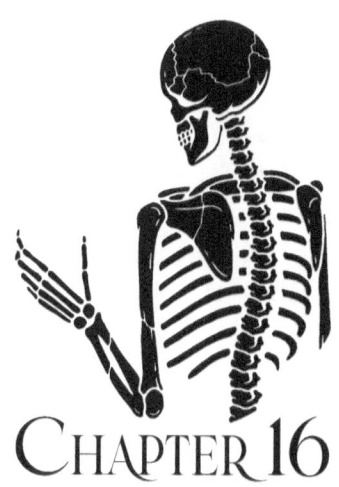

CHAPTER 16

The alarm clock chimed several times before I woke to Zeba licking my hair. I pet her head then got up and headed for the shower. I turned it on hot and jumped in, finally my body came alive.

I got dressed and headed to the kitchen to get coffee. Little Cobb was laying in the middle of the kitchen floor eating my leftovers he had knocked the box off the table and was sitting in the box crunching away at a chip.

"Bad Slinky!" I told him as I picked him up.

I put him by his bowl and handed him the rest of the chip. Then cleaned up the mess he made, chips and chicken were all over the place. So much for leftovers for lunch I thought to myself. I made myself a big cup of coffee and dumped lots of sugar in it and milk. I was mentally going over what I was going to say to Lulu's family. When I got it worked out I picked up the phone and placed the call to them.

It rang several times before an answer, then, "Hallo? This is Kalapriya who's this?" she asked.

"Yes, my name is Rainey, I'm the one who bought Lulu's skeleton for my class room. The donor company gave me your number." I told her as if she didn't already know where I got the number.

"Yes, been expecting a call from you. What is it that you needed to know?"

"Well, I was wondering if she donated herself or if your family donated her?" I questioned her.

"We donated the both of them after she and the baby passed away due to large amounts of debts to hospital."

I shook my head. Did she just say a baby too?

"You mean there was a baby donated too?"

"Yes, Lulu died when there were complications with the birth of her baby girl. The baby was a breach and the Dr. couldn't deliver the baby fast enough, the baby suffocated in the birth canal when the cord wrapped around her neck."

I sat there for a minute, and then said, "How terrible. That was, and how sorry I was for their losses."

"Yes, it was terrible but Lulu and the baby, Khali, will spend all eternity together now."

"What do you mean?" I questioned her.

"Yes, we donated them both so they would be sold together. The company assured us."

I cleared my throat then said, "I only have Lulu, not her and the baby. I knew nothing of the baby till now."

She started crying then speaking in her language, and then finally said, "You must get the baby so Lulu can rest."

"Of course I will do whatever it takes to bring them together for her to be at peace. I will reunite them."

I assured them that I would work it out and would call when I had the problem fixed. I too wanted Lulu and the baby to be together.

"Thank you. Call when the baby is with you. I will wait to hear from you."

I assured her again then hung up. No wonder Lulu's not at peace, I probably wouldn't be if I was her either. It was all so sad I thought about it for a few minutes then I made a call to the company Exoskeleton. I figured the baby was still there waiting to be sold.

I grabbed the folder with the company's number in it then dialed, on the second ring a woman picked up the phone.

"Yes, I need to know if this particular skeleton is still available for sale."

"Sure, I can look that up. What is the name of it?" she asked me.

"The name is Khali, and she came in with another skeleton named, Lulu and they were supposed to be sold together. Lulu's number is 4242."

"It will take a minute for it to come up on the computer please hold."

As I sat on hold I was silently praying that they would find Khali and I could reunite them. After a few minutes the lady picked up the phone and asked for the number again that Lulu was under. I gave it to her and then she informed me, "Yes, I've located Khali and she is still available for sale. Would you like to purchase her today?"

"YES!" I said into the phone; I was so happy!

I grabbed my purse and took out my credit card.

"I have my credit card ready when you are," I said to her.

I read off the numbers of the card to her then she said, "It will take a week or so to ship. The card went through without problems. Is there anything else I can do for you?"

I thanked her and said, "No, that's all I needed? Oh, when will it be delivered?"

"Right on Halloween day its due."

"Thank you so much, goodbye."

And with that she hung up.

I was so excited I forgot what time it was, I had to be to school in twenty minutes. I hustled and ran out the door. I got there and the second bell had just ringed, not late today. When the class was all settled down I made the announcement that we would be getting a baby skeleton that was Lulu's baby and we needed to start collecting cans again to pay for her. That way I'd get paid back for buying her.

The baby wasn't as expensive as Lulu was but still she was a lot. It was worth buying her so that the haunting would stop though. I shared the whole story with the class. They all thought that once they were reunited that everything would go back to normal again. I agreed with them and crossed my fingers.

The school day flew by, and before I left, I told Lulu that I found her baby and that she would be coming here soon to join her. I turned to get Lulu's shawl to cover her up and when I turned around on the board it said, "Thank you."

I told her that she was welcome and that I was sorry she and Khali got separated. When she was wrapped up, I was ready to go home. I turned off the lights and walked down the hallway. I went to the office to run off a few papers and I ran into Jet grabbing her mail.

I told her what I had found out and that I ordered the baby. Jet was so happy for me; she said that maybe all the strange occurrences would settle down after the baby arrived. I agreed and told her I hoped so. I said goodnight and headed home. I was so happy I jammed with Bob Marley all the way home, it is such happy music.

As soon as I walked into the house I grabbed the house phone and called Charlie to tell him the exciting news. He didn't answer so I left him a long message. He'd call me back later. Little Cobb came hopping into the kitchen so I picked him up and told him the good news as I petted his cute little ears.

He chirped at me and I knew he was as happy as I was. So I hugged him and put him down by his food bowl. I put in a piece of peppermint stick for him, he loved them. I relaxed for the rest of the night out back in the garden until it got dark.

Just as I opened the door the phone was ringing, it was Charlie. I talked with him for a long time, and then after I explained it all to him. He said that it was all going to work out and that Lulu would be at peace once the baby was at her side.

At least that was the plan we hoped for. We said goodnight and hung up. I ate a peanut butter and honey sandwich then headed upstairs to read. I fell into a deep sleep soon after that. I dreamed of Lulu and Khali, it was a pleasant dream and they seemed at peace.

Lulu thanked me and I woke just as she was hugging me. I was happy that they seemed content in the dream. I hoped in real life it would be the same.

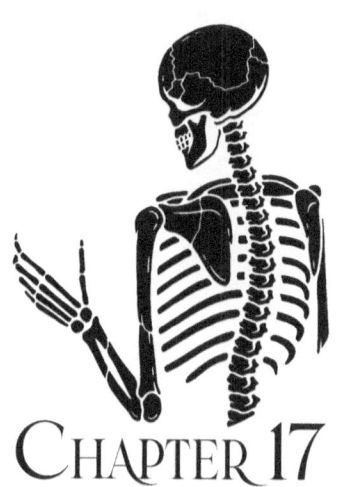

CHAPTER 17

Two weeks fly by, and it was the week of Halloween, the baby Khali had arrived that morning. I hung her next to Lulu so they could be by each other. I had dressed up Lulu for the occasion; she was dressed in an orange India dress and a sari on her head.

Today the school photographer was coming to our room to take a picture of the class with Lulu and the baby for a story in the school paper. Our class was all dressed up for the Halloween picture.

After lunch, the photographer came to take our picture and we all gathered around Lulu and Khali. She took several photos so that she could pick the best one later. After a few minutes she said she had what she needed and thanked us all.

The next day was Halloween, so when I came into the classroom and found Lulu with Khali in a sling hanging from her shoulder I wasn't surprised. They had both died on that day one year ago. They looked very cute together so I left them like that for the day. Several of the kids commented on it, but we all thought it was wonderful seeing them together.

By lunchtime the school newspaper came out, prefect timing the Halloween addition. I bought a copy then headed for the teachers lounge to read it while I ate. I turned to our class's story and read it through. When I looked at the picture, I couldn't believe it- in the corner standing by me was Lulu holding Khali in her arms!

The photographer got a picture of her and the baby's ghost on film! She looked beautiful and happy; she had a huge smile on her face. After a year of turmoil Lulu and Khali were at peace finally.

REFERENCES

Aileen Wuornos- Murderpedia.com
Serial killers the world's most evil by Nigel Blundell
Wikipedia.org, true crimes serial killers.com
Psycho USA by Harrold Schechter
The new predator women who kill
Profiles of female serial killers by Dr Deborah Schurman-Kauflin
Murderpedia- The Encyclopedia of Murderers-Hunting humans
MargBousun - NYDailynews.com
The Devils Rooming House by M. William Phelps
The Fatal Women – Mystery of seven infants death by Paris Dailymail (London England May 11, 1908)
Truetv.com
Top 10 deadiest female killers-toptenz.net
More than horror, serial killers, biography,books,dvd
http://disturbinghorror.com/serial-killers/serial-killers-bio/belle-gunness.html
Married"Em and Burried "em".Idahostatesman,the (Bosose,Id) Tuesday July 9, 2002,life,03retrieved november 3,2008, from America:news bank database
Lady Bluebreard:The True Story of Love and Marriage, death by Anderson, William C About.comcrime/punishment
The Worlds Worst Criminals-an A-Z of Evil Men and Women by Charolotte Greig
The Correggio soap-,maker(http://www.museocriminologico.it/correggio-uk.htm)
http://www.time.com/time/magizine/artical109718528400.00html)
Inside the Mind of Casey Anthony By Keith Ablow,M.D.
Wicked Intentions-The Shelia LaBarre Murders By Kevin Flynn

I Monster-Serial Killers in their own chilling words by Tom Philbin
"The Fatal Women'mystery of seven infants deaths"
More Than Horror,SerialKiller,Biography,Books,dvd.com
http://distrubinghorror.com/Serial-Killers/Serial-Killers-Bio/Belle-Gunness.html
About.com Crime/PunishmentWomen who kill.com
Andrea Yates video resultsEvil women.com
Profile of Andrea Yates
Andrea Yates child killer/evil ladies.com
(http://www.time.com/time.com/time/magizine/artical/0,9171,766205,00.html)
America:Newsbank database http://query.nytimes.com/gst/abstract.html?
http://www.findagrave.com
The Unknown History of Misandry.com
"Fatal:The Poisionous Life of a Female Serial Killer" by Harrold Schecter
"The encyclopedia of Serial Killers" by Lane, Brian and Greg,Wilfred
TrueTv's Crime Library(http://www.truev.com/library/crime/serial-killers/weird/vampires/4.html)
www.crime library entry
"The Case of Mary Bell" by Gitta Sereny
The Creepest Female Serial Killers
The Witch of Vladimirovac
"Tainted Legacy: The Story of Alleged Serial Killer Bertha Gifford" by Kay
Murphy
"The Lizzy Borden Sourcebook" by David Kent
"The World's Most Mysterious Murders" by Patrica Fanthorpe and Lionel
Fanthorpe
Findagrave.com-LizzyBorden
"The Most Evil Men and Women in History" by Miranda Twiss
Nazi-Ilse koch.com
Ilse Koch the Bitch Of Buchenwald
www.Hitlerschildren.com
Judith Neelley crime library.com

Judith Neelley The Trial
Serial Killer Judith Neelley documentary-utube
Serialkillercalendar.com
People.famouswhy.com/dortheapuente
Mary Tudor- evil bloody mary/evil ladies.com
Europeanhistory.about.com
www.crimelibrary.com/serial-killer/predator/bathoryInfamouslady.com

www.ingramcontent.com/pod-product-compliance
Lightning Source LLC
LaVergne TN
LVHW091557060526
838200LV00036B/875